Echoes of Yesterday

Randy Harper

Contents

Chapter 1

The bar was noisy, full of people talking, laughing, and the occasional clink of glasses. Somewhere in the background, a guitar was strumming, almost lost in the mix. I leaned back, beer in hand, and just watched my friends messing around, cracking up over something stupid. They were cracking jokes, swapping stories, voices blending into the noise, like it was all part of the same song. You could smell grilled food in the air, mixed with the sharp, familiar tang of alcohol. The place was dim, but it had that warm, laid-back vibe I loved.

Aeon was across the table, bright-eyed and all smiles, nodding along while one of our colleagues told a story about some silly mistake at work. I could see her glance my way every now and then, her eyes kind of twinkling with that playful look she always had. It was like she wanted to pull me into the conversation, but I was happy just sitting there, sipping my drink, letting the night drift by.

The band wrapped up their set, and then the speakers kicked in. A few seconds later, I heard the familiar chords of an Itchyworms song. I couldn't help but grin. "Alright! Lets go!" I said, nudging Jay, who was slouched next to me. "Now it feels like a real night out."

He rolled his eyes. "Really, man? Can't you get tired of this band? They play the same songs every time we're here."

I shook my head, chuckling. "Nope. This is comfort food for my ears. No matter how messed up your day gets, you hear these songs, and it's like everything just... clicks." I raised my bottle, almost as if I was toasting to the music.

Aeon leaned in, elbows on the table, her lips curling into a smile. "You've always been like that, Jack. Stubbornly loyal to your favorites. It's kind of... cute," she teased, her eyes meeting mine for a moment longer than necessary.

I laughed, raising my beer in mock offense. "Hey, loyalty is a virtue, right?"

She rolled her eyes but kept that smile. "Yeah, but when you're playing the same songs over and over, it can drive other people crazy. Like, seriously, this is like the fourth time tonight I've heard Beer in this place. They're trying to tell us something."

I shrugged, still grinning. "Maybe they're just giving us what we need-a reason to sing along. No complications, no pressure. Just a good time."

Jay raised his drink. "I'll drink that. Here's to no complications."

We all clinked bottles, and as we took a sip, I felt Aeon's foot nudge mine under the table. She had that same soft look in her eyes. "I get it, though," she said, just loud enough for me to hear over the music. "Sometimes you just need something familiar to cling to when everything else feels... unpredictable."

I caught her eye and felt a pang of something. It was hard to explain-appreciation, maybe, or something deeper. I quickly brushed it off and chuckled. "Exactly. That's why Itchyworms will always be on my playlist."

Aeon's smile grew wider as she tapped her fingers on the table, syncing with the song's rhythm. "That's why you're my favorite, Jack. You're simple. Predictable, but in a good way."

I raised an eyebrow, smirking. "Simple? I'm hurt," I said, laughing. It was always like this between us, light and easy.

The conversation flowed, and soon enough, so did the drinks. The jokes got louder, the laughter warmer, and the night felt like it would never end. The Itchyworms played on, as if they were setting the mood for us. For a while, everything felt uncomplicated, like nothing could go wrong.

Then my phone buzzed in my pocket. Dina's name lit up the screen. I glanced around the table; everyone was still caught up in their own chatter.

I paused, then picked up the call. "Hey, babe... yeah, we're almost done. Just one last song, I promise."

There was a soft laugh on the other end, the kind that made me smile without even realizing it. "You said that thirty minutes ago," Dina teased, her voice warm and gentle. "You know how late it is. Do I need to pick you up? I'll use my wheelchair."

I glanced at my watch, wincing slightly. She was right; we'd been here longer than I'd intended. "I know, I know. I'm sorry. I just lost track of time," I said, trying to sound sincere and playful at the same time. "We're just unwinding after work."

"Is Aeon there?" she asked, her tone shifting just slightly.

I could hear the hint of tension in her voice. "Yeah, she's with us," I replied, trying to keep my tone light. "We're just catching up, you know?"

"Mm-hmm," she said, a hint of something unspoken lingering between us. "Just make sure you don't drink too much, okay? I need you to get home safely."

"I will. I promise," I said, feeling a small pang of guilt. I didn't mean to worry her, but I also didn't want to leave just yet. It was rare that the three of us had the chance to unwind together like this, and I knew Jay and Aeon felt the same. "I'll be home soon."

"Alright," she sighed, but I could hear the smile in her voice. "Just don't make me wait too long."

I chuckled, the sound easing the tension I hadn't realized was building in my chest. "I won't. Love you."

"Love you too," she said, and with that, the call ended, leaving me staring at my phone for a moment longer.

Aeon leaned back in her chair, watching me with a knowing smirk. "Smart woman," she said, taking a sip of her drink. "Doesn't want you getting too carried away."

I rolled my eyes, but I couldn't help but smile. "She worries too much. But that's just her way of showing she cares."

"Or maybe she's just trying to keep you out of trouble," Aeon teased, her smile playful but her eyes thoughtful. "You never know."

I let out a quick laugh, but I could feel the teasing starting to take on a different tone. Finishing off the rest of my beer, I grabbed my helmet from the chair next to me and stood up. "Alright, I'm heading out. Gotta keep the wife happy."

"Already?" Jay said, his face dropping a bit. "Come on, man, the night's still young!"

"Yeah, but so am I, and I'd like to stay that way," I replied with a grin. "Besides, I'm thinking of grabbing something for Dina on the way home. Maybe her favorite ice cream. A peace offering."

Aeon's smile flickered for a moment, but she quickly hid it behind a smirk. "Aww, how sweet. Trying to score some extra points, huh?"

"Something like that," I said, slipping my helmet under my arm. "See you guys next time."

"Just be careful out there, Jack," Aeon said, her voice softening. "I mean it."

I nodded, then waved to the others as I stepped outside. The cool night air hit me, and I took a deep breath, letting the last notes of Itchyworms drift away. I pulled out my phone to see if any convenience stores were still open, intending to grab Dina's favorite ice cream.

Walking towards the parking lot, the cool night air felt rejuvenating on my skin. I had reached the halfway point when I noticed footsteps approaching from behind. Whirling around, I saw Aeon rushing to keep pace, the noise of her heels echoing on the sidewalk.

"Leaving without saying goodbye properly?" she teased, her smile playful.

I raised an eyebrow, amused. "I thought I already did that back there."

"Not exactly," she replied, pausing a couple of paces before me, close enough for me to catch a hint of mischief in her eyes. "I thought I'd walk you to your bike. Make sure you don't change your mind and come back for another round."

I chuckled, shaking my head. "I'm done for the night, Aeon. Dina's waiting for me."

"Dina, Dina, Dina..." she said, rolling her eyes but still smiling. "You always bring her up." She hesitated for a moment, then added, "Makes a girl feel a little left out, you know?"

I knew she was being playful, but there was something about her tone that made my heart skip a beat. Aeon was always quick with a clever line, light-hearted and easygoing, but tonight I could sense a hint of something else-something that felt almost vulnerable.

"I mean, you know it's not like that," I said, trying to keep my tone casual. "Dina's my wife."

"Yeah, yeah, I know," she said, her voice softening as she took a small step closer. "But can she make you laugh like I can?"

I hesitated, unsure of how to respond. "You're different, Aeon. You're... you."

She smirked, tilting her head. "Good answer. But you're still dodging the question."

Before I could say anything, she continued, "You know, we're pretty lucky. Not everyone gets to work with their best friends from college. Who'd have thought we'd all end up at the same company? From jamming in Jay's garage to corporate meetings... life's weird, huh?"

"Yeah, it is," I said, smiling at the thought. "From making music to making presentations... It's not what I expected, but I'm glad we're still together."

"I'm glad, too," she said, her voice a little softer. "Even if things didn't work out exactly like we planned." Her eyes lingered on mine for a moment, and I knew she wasn't just talking about our careers.

Aeon and I had a past-one that started with late-night practice sessions, writing songs, and shared dreams of making it big. It didn't last, but we managed to stay friends, even after everything changed. Still, there were times, like now, when I could see a flicker of something unresolved in her eyes.

I cleared my throat, trying to steer the conversation back. "Anyway, I really should get going. I promised Dina I'd grab her some ice cream on the way."

"Of course," she said, her playful smile returning. "Always the perfect husband." But her eyes softened, and she added, "Just remember, if you ever need a break from all that sweetness... I'm still here to stir things up."

I didn't know how to respond, so I just smiled, hoping it was enough. Aeon's face softened as she took a step back, giving a little wave. "Have a good night, Jack. Ride safe."

"You too, Aeon. See you next week?" I asked, trying to sound casual.

"Maybe," she said, her smile widening as she looked at me for a moment longer. "If I'm not too busy missing you."

I laughed and shook my head before heading to my bike. As I strapped on my helmet, her words echoed in my head, leaving me with a strange, uneasy feeling. I glanced back to see her still standing there, barely visible in the dim light of the parking lot, watching me as I started the engine.

I got on my motorcycle, sensing the familiar vibration as I turned on the engine. Rain started to drizzle lightly, then gradually intensified. I turned on my playlist, and before long, Itchyworms was serenading me once more, their music enveloping the area like a familiar companion.

Chapter 2

I accelerated the motorbike engine and drove out of the parking lot, feeling the cool night breeze on my face. The streets were generally silent, with the occasional sound of a car horn breaking the quietness. When I gave Dina the ice cream, I could already envision her smiling. I thought it might help alleviate the tension from our previous conversation, even if it was just a small gesture.

Upon nearing the ice cream shop, I noticed a blinking neon sign. The dark was aglow with the inviting light of "Sweet Indulgence". I left my bike and entered the building, feeling the refreshing breeze as the delightful aroma of vanilla and sugar surrounded me.

The interior of the shop was unexpectedly bustling for a late-night spot to grab a snack. I observed a woman in front of a freezer packed with big containers of ice cream as a line curved around the counter. Her flowing hair was long and she wore a vibrant sundress that appeared to reflect the light. I observed her carefully considering the tastes, her fingers delicately touching the containers.

Approaching, I caught her talking to the cashier." I want to buy the last Mango Ube Delight container, please."

I felt disheartened when I realized I also craved that taste. "Sorry, but is that the Mango Ube Delight?" I inquired, attempting to appear nonchalant despite the urgency in my tone.

She looked in my direction, and our gazes locked. Her gaze held a captivating quality, giving the impression that she could see into my soul. "Being," she responded, with a mischievous grin on her face. However, it appears that you are just a brief instant behind.

I stopped, feeling a strange connection. "I admitted to being very enthusiastic about that particular one," I said, my disappointment evident.

Raising an eyebrow, her expression changed subtly. "Sometimes, not getting something could actually be a blessing in disguise." There was a suggestion of hidden knowledge in her voice, indicating she knew more than she revealed.

"What are you trying to say?" I inquired, intrigued.

She continued with a slight shrug, "Imagine if you were given the opportunity to experience something new?" "A brand new world where you could obtain whatever you desired?" The air was filled with her words, sending a shiver down my back.

I chuckled uneasily, attempting to ignore the strangeness of the conversation. "Seems like a dream, doesn't it?"

"Maybe," she answered, her stare remaining steady. However, there are occasions when fantasy can materialize in ways that are unforeseen. You never know what surprises life might bring.

At that moment, the cashier gave her the final container of Mango Ube Delight. With a pleased smile, she accepted it and then faced me. "Have fun exploring ice cream," she whispered mysteriously as she left, leaving her lingering like a pleasant fragrance.

I remained in confusion following our conversation. With my head shaking, I walked up to the counter and was welcomed by the cashier with a smile. "What may I offer you?"

"I'll take a tub of vanilla, thanks," I said, still preoccupied with the odd interaction. While I waited, I couldn't rid myself of the sense that the woman had hidden depths.

Walking back outside with my container of vanilla ice cream, I felt the refreshing chill of the night air serving as a wake-up call. Her words echoed ominously as I replayed the encounter in my mind. Once again, I chuckled it away, but a strong feeling inside me told me to take notice.

After mounting my motorcycle, I looked back at the shop, but the woman had disappeared. I inhaled deeply, ignoring the strangeness and refocusing on my task. HOME. I needed to resolve things with Dina.

I turned on the engine, allowing the usual sound to occupy the silent night, and drove onto the street.

While I was moving along the streets, the initial raindrops started to descend, gentle at the beginning and hardly discernible. However, in just a few minutes, it transformed into a consistent downpour. The lights of the city became hazy as I looked through my visor, with raindrops forming small patterns that twirled and glowed.

Despite the heavy rain obstructing my view, I persevered in order to reach my destination. I pictured Dina lying on the couch, eagerly anticipating my arrival. I wished the ice cream would bring a smile to her face, possibly even a chuckle, as I tried to make amends for coming home late.

"Persevere" I laughingly whispered thinking such a deep word came from my mouth , holding onto the handlebars more firmly while the rain poured down heavily. The roads were wet, mirroring the shining red and yellow of traffic signals, and I sensed the chill penetrate my coat.

The rain intensified, hammering on my helmet, creating a sense of distance and muffled sounds in my surroundings. Despite the world becoming blurry, I maintained my focus on the road, with my only thoughts being about reaching home to see Dina. As I raced through the wet streets, my playlist continued to play, and I heard the familiar tune of Di Na Muli, its initial notes softly reverberating in my ears.

The music created an unusual feeling of tranquility, resembling a lullaby, while the rain kept pouring down. It was a song I had played over and over again, bringing back a mix of joy and sadness. I quietly hummed along, allowing the music to lead me while maneuvering the slick road.

As I rounded a corner, the road was suddenly illuminated by the bright glare of headlights. I felt a sudden jolt in my chest as I attempted to swerve, hearing the sound of tires skidding on the wet pavement. Everything transpired quickly—the bright lights, the deafening sound of a horn.

In that split second, my mind raced back to the strange encounter I had at the ice cream shop. The woman with the flowing hair and the playful smile had said something that lingered with me, echoing in my thoughts as the headlights bore down. "What if you had the chance to explore something different? A whole new world where you could have anything you wanted?" Her words danced in my mind, sending shivers down my spine.

Could there really be another reality out there, a place where I wouldn't be stuck in the same old routine? I remembered the way her eyes sparkled with mischief as she spoke, as if she held secrets about the universe. What did she mean by a new world? Was it possible to escape the troubles I faced?

At that moment, it felt like I was standing at a crossroads, teetering between the life I knew and the unknown possibilities she hinted at. What if I didn't have to rush home? What if I could linger a bit longer, enjoying the playful banter with Aeon? The thought of staying, of flirting and getting lost in her infectious laughter, tugged at my heart.

Her smile had always held a certain allure, a spark that ignited something deep within me. I could almost picture us sharing jokes, the tension between us bubbling under the surface, creating a delicious thrill that was hard to ignore. What if I embraced that connection? It was a fleeting thought, but the idea of a life where I could explore that chemistry—free from the weight of responsibility—tempted me more than I cared to admit.

But then there was Dina, my anchor, the warmth of her love grounding me. I couldn't abandon her, no matter how enticing the flirtation with Aeon felt.

Suddenly, my mind flashed back to that night at the bar, long before Dina and I were anything more than strangers. The place had been packed, the dim lights casting a warm, intimate glow over the crowd. It was the kind of atmosphere that made you feel like the world outside didn't exist, where worries melted away with every strum of the guitar.

I was up on stage with Jay and Aeon, our little college band doing a set of covers, mostly Itchyworms songs. We weren't professionals, but we had a decent following in the local scene—just enough to make nights like this feel like something special. We'd been playing for almost an hour when I caught sight of her, standing near the bar with a group of friends, her smile bright and carefree as if she owned the night.

I remember stumbling over a chord when our eyes met. She was radiant, her laughter lighting up the room, and in that instant, I felt an inexplicable pull—like I'd been yanked out of the song and into her orbit. She noticed me staring, and for a moment, our gazes locked. I could feel my heart skip a beat, the world around us blurring, leaving just her—this beautiful, vibrant girl in the middle of a noisy bar.

We continued our set, but my focus kept drifting back to her. She was swaying to the music, her movements graceful, almost hypnotic. I wanted to keep playing, just to see her smile. As we finished our cover of "Akin Ka Na Lang," I turned to Aeon, hoping she hadn't noticed how distracted I was. But she had—of course, she had. Aeon could read me like a book. She shot me a knowing look, her eyes narrowing, and gave a subtle shake of her head, as if warning me not to get too caught up.

During our break, I grabbed a drink and tried to compose myself, but I kept glancing her way. To my surprise, she caught my eye again and smiled, a playful, inviting smile that sent a jolt of excitement through me. I felt a tap on my shoulder, and there was Aeon, holding out a bottle of water. "Careful, Jack," she said, her tone light but her eyes serious. "You're staring."

"I wasn't—" I began, but she cut me off with a smirk.

"Yeah, you were," she said, glancing over at Dina, who was still chatting with her friends. "She's cute. But don't get any ideas. We've got a gig to finish, and you know how this goes."

I knew what she meant. Aeon had always been protective, a little too much sometimes, especially since we had history—brief but intense. We'd dated for a while in college, a relationship that had burned hot and fast before fizzling out. Still, we managed to stay close, and she'd become like a constant in my life. Maybe that's why she felt the need to warn me off. But that night, I wasn't thinking about the past or the band. I was thinking about the girl at the bar who had just made my world tilt on its axis.

When we got back on stage, I played with a different energy, pouring my focus into every note, every lyric, hoping she'd stay to hear it. I sang "Beer" with a grin, almost laughing when I saw her raise a glass in response, her friends cheering. It was a small interaction, but it felt like a spark—one I didn't want to lose.

As we wrapped up our set, I glanced at Aeon, who was watching me carefully, a faint line of concern creasing her brow. I knew she saw it too—the connection that was forming, and the way I was being drawn in. For a second, I thought she might say something, try to distract me, but she didn't. Instead, she turned back to her guitar, strumming the opening chords of our last song, letting it play out.

The gig ended, and as the applause died down, I found myself drifting toward the bar. I didn't have a plan—just a need to see her up close, to hear her voice. When I finally approached, she turned to me, eyes bright with curiosity.

"Hey," I said, feeling absurdly nervous for a guy who had just performed in front of a crowd. "Did you... enjoy the set?"

She laughed, a light, musical sound that made my heart swell. "Yeah, you guys were great! Especially you," she said, tilting her head, her eyes twinkling. "You looked like you were having a lot of fun up there."

"I was," I admitted, feeling my cheeks warm. "More than usual, actually."

We talked for a while, her friends drifting off one by one until it was just the two of us. I learned that her name was Dina, and she was as easy to talk to as she was to look at. We shared stories, jokes, and at some point, she mentioned she loved Itchyworms, which made me grin. "Then you've got good taste," I said, earning another laugh.

Out of the corner of my eye, I saw Aeon watching from across the room, her expression unreadable. I knew she'd sensed what was happening, and part of me felt a pang of guilt, but I also knew I couldn't walk away from this. The night felt like one of those rare moments where everything aligns perfectly, and I didn't want to let it slip away.

We exchanged numbers before the night was over, and as I headed back to the stage to pack up, I could still feel the buzz of that first connection, the kind that makes you believe in fate, or destiny, or whatever it is that makes two people meet at the right place and the right time. Aeon said nothing as we loaded up our gear, but I caught the way her eyes flicked between me and Dina, as if trying to gauge how serious I was.

That night marked the beginning of something I hadn't seen coming. It was the start of a journey that would change every-thing—not just for me, but for all of us. And even now, as the memory played out in my mind, I could still feel the thrill of that first spark, the one that ignited the path that led us here.

Yet, as the headlights loomed closer, that pull toward something different—a chance to indulge in a moment of carefree joy—clashed violently with the reality of my commitments. And then, in an instant, the moment shattered. A loud noise erupted—the sound of metal smashing and breaking, drowning out everything else—followed by an unsettling silence. The music cut off, leaving only the steady and relentless sound of the rain as darkness descended.

In those fleeting seconds before everything went dark, I felt a pang of regret that cut deeper than any physical pain. I hadn't even seen her face light up as she took the first scoop of ice cream, hadn't experienced the joy of sharing that small pleasure with her. The thought gnawed at me, a relentless ache that twisted in my gut.

"Dina," I whispered into the void, my voice lost in the chaos. "If only I could turn back time... just to see you smile again." A desperate plea, an unfulfilled wish. In that instant, I realized how much I would give to grasp that moment again, to live it over just to see her take that bite of ice cream, to hear her laughter ring out like a sweet melody one more time.

Chapter 3

My eyes snapped open, and I wasn't greeted by the familiar sight of my bedroom or the cold, sterile walls of a hospital room. Instead, I found myself standing in a strange, ethereal place—a domain that seemed to exist outside of reality. It was unlike anything I had ever seen. The sky was a deep, endless indigo, speckled with soft, shimmering lights that pulsed gently, like a heartbeat. There was no horizon, just an infinite expanse of space stretching in every direction, as if the world itself had been painted on a canvas of night.

I was standing on what seemed to be a path made of dark, reflective stone, shimmering like black pearls under the faint, silvery glow. Surrounding the path were delicate, ghostly tendrils of mist, drifting and swirling, creating shapes that were there one moment and gone the next. It felt both serene and unsettling, like I was walking through a dream that had somehow taken on a life of its own.

"What is this place?" I murmured, my voice barely a whisper, but the mist around me seemed to catch my words, carrying them off into the dark. I tried to move, but every step felt slow and deliberate, like the world was holding its breath, waiting.

Then I felt it—a subtle shift in the air, like a ripple spreading out across a still pond. The mist gathered and twisted ahead of me, coalescing into a shape, until a figure began to emerge. Slowly, an old woman took form, her silhouette outlined by the soft, pale light that seemed to emanate from somewhere deep within her. She was draped in flowing robes, dark and fluid, decorated with intricate patterns that glimmered like constellations. Her long, silver hair moved gently, as if stirred by a breeze I couldn't feel, and her eyes... her eyes glowed like the moon itself, bright and ancient.

"Who are you?" I asked, my voice cracking a little, the sound echoing softly through the misty expanse.

She tilted her head slightly, a faint smile touching her lips. "I have been known by many names," she said, her voice smooth, almost musical, like the gentle hum of wind through leaves. "But you may call me Mayari."

The name struck a chord deep within me, like a half-remembered story from a time long gone. Mayari—the goddess of the moon, a symbol of rebirth and transformation. I'd heard her name in folklore, in tales whispered late at night. But this couldn't be real. "Mayari..." I repeated, trying to wrap my head around it. "What... what do you want from me?"

She stepped closer, and with each step, the mist seemed to part, revealing more of her domain. I could see what looked like ancient stone pillars rising from the ground, adorned with moonflowers that glowed softly, illuminating the space with a gentle, ethereal light. "It is not what I want, Jack. It is what you desire," she said, her gaze unwavering, piercing. "You called out, didn't you? You pleaded to turn back the hands of time, to undo the sorrow that now weighs heavy on your heart."

My chest tightened. "If this is a dream, I want to wake up," I said, trying to sound firm, but my voice trembled. "I want to go back to my life."

Mayari's expression softened, but there was something in her eyes—an understanding that felt almost painful to look at. "You wish to return, but to what? You were struck by a truck; you'd be in a vegetative state at best. Dina would be heartbroken. You would have nothing to return to."

"I want to go back to Dina," I said, desperation creeping into my voice. "I want to see her again."

Mayari's gaze shimmered with a depth of wisdom and compassion. "And you can, but it comes at a price."

My head snapped up, hope and caution twisting together inside me. "A price? What do you mean?"

She raised her hand, and the mist around us rippled, shifting and swirling until images began to form, flickering and fading like reflections on water. I saw Dina, her smile, her laughter, the way she could light up a room just by being there. I saw the music, the songs that used to mean everything to me, and my friends—Aeon and Jay—who were always there, even when everything else felt like it was falling apart. Each image felt like a punch to the gut, a reminder of everything I was clinging to.

"The price is not one you can measure in gold or silver," she said. "It is far more precious. If you wish to turn back time, to change your fate, you must be willing to lose something you hold dear."

I felt my pulse quicken. "I can't... I can't trade a life for a life. I'm not willing to sacrifice someone else just to get her back."

Mayari's lips twitched into a sad, almost knowing smile. "I am not asking for a life. No one will die. But something much more will be lost—something that exists not as flesh and blood, but as an idea, a presence in the world."

I frowned, trying to make sense of her words. "What are you talking about?"

The images shifted again, this time showing the band—me, Aeon, and Jay, on a stage, playing to a crowd. I could almost hear the music, the familiar chords, feel the rush of being up there, the way the audience would cheer, like we were all connected by an invisible thread.

"You see, Jack," she continued, her voice soft and melodic, "there are things in this world that hold power—not just because they exist, but because of the impact they have, the way they shape people's lives, bring them together, inspire them. The music you created with your friends was one such thing."

My throat tightened, my heart pounding. "What does this have to do with Dina?"

"The world you wish to return to," she said, her voice barely above a whisper, "will require a change—something fundamental, a shift that will alter the fabric of reality. You wish to erase the pain, to reclaim what was lost, but to do so means something else must be undone, taken away. A balance must be maintained."

The images dissolved, leaving just the two of us, her eyes never leaving mine. "What would be lost?" I asked, barely able to get the words out.

"Something will be missing, Jack. Something that has shaped your life, your experiences, and your connection to those you love. A sacrifice is needed for a new beginning."

I felt like I was spinning, the ground—if there was any—slipping away beneath me. "Why... why does it have to be this way?"

She placed a hand on my shoulder, her touch gentle, almost comforting. "Because every choice has consequences, Jack. Every wish has a price. You can walk away from this dream, return to your life as it is, or you can take this chance to rewrite your story. But understand, the world you will return to will be a different one, shaped by what you are willing to sacrifice."

I closed my eyes, feeling the suffocating weight of the decision. The mist around us seemed to close in, pressing against my chest, and for the first time, I felt truly, utterly alone.

Suddenly, I was pulled from the present and plunged into a vivid memory. The colors around me shifted, swirling into familiar shapes, until I found myself sitting on the couch in our small apartment. The walls were adorned with photographs capturing our lives, moments of laughter and warmth. The air was thick with the scent of comfort food—Dina's specialty, adobo—cooking in the kitchen.

I glanced over, watching her as she hummed softly to herself, stirring the pot with a wooden spoon. Her long hair fell in waves over her shoulder, framing her face with a kind of radiance that always made my heart swell. But I could also see the worry in her eyes, the slight crease in her brow that hinted at the burden she was trying to shield me from.

"Jack," she called out, her voice soft yet filled with a strength that seemed to cut through my dark thoughts. "You okay?"

I forced a smile, but I could feel the weight of my sadness pushing down on me. "Yeah, just a little tired."

She turned to face me fully, concern etched across her features. "You've been working so hard. You don't have to do it all alone, you know."

The honesty in her words struck a chord. I had been struggling, consumed by a sense of hopelessness, but I was never truly alone. She had always been there, a steadfast anchor in the turbulent waters of my emotions. Even in my darkest moments, when despair threatened to pull me under, Dina was the light that guided me back.

"Remember that song we used to listen to?" she said, leaning against the counter, her eyes sparkling with nostalgia. "'Huwag Na Sana 'Kong Gumising Mag-Isa'? I always loved how it reminds us that we're better together."

I chuckled softly, recalling the lyrics, the way they spoke of companionship, of not wanting to wake up alone. It resonated with me deeply, especially in times when my mind spiraled into the depths of loneliness. "Yeah, I remember. It's a good song."

Dina approached me, her gaze steady. "You don't have to carry everything by yourself, Jack. I'm here, and I'll always be here. Even when things get hard, just remember that."

Her words wrapped around me like a warm embrace, chasing away the shadows lurking in my mind. "I know," I whispered, the lump in my throat rising. "I just... I feel like I'm not enough sometimes."

"You are more than enough," she insisted, her voice firm but filled with love. "We'll face everything together. You're not alone in this, and you never will be."

As I watched her, I felt the depth of my emotions swell. She was my light, my reason to keep going. In that moment, the weight on my shoulders began to lift. The darkness didn't seem as daunting when she was beside me, a constant reminder that I had someone who cared deeply.

Suddenly, the memory began to fade, the colors swirling back into the mist. I fought against it, desperate to hold onto the warmth of her presence, the strength she had given me when I felt lost. But as I was pulled back into the ethereal domain, the realization hit me like a cold wave—what if I lost that connection? What if I lost her?

Back in the present, Mayari stood before me, her gaze unwavering. I took a shaky breath, determination surging within me. I didn't want to wake up alone; I didn't want to lose the love that had pulled me from despair time and time again.

"I'll take the deal," I said, my voice steadier than I felt. "I want to go back with Dina."

Mayari nodded, a flicker of understanding in her eyes. "Very well, Jack. But remember, every choice has its consequences. You may regain what you lost, but something else will inevitably vanish."

I felt the weight of my decision settle on my shoulders, yet the thought of being with Dina again eclipsed my fears. I was ready to face whatever came next, determined to hold onto the love that had always saved me.

Chapter 4

Mayari stepped closer, her presence radiating a warmth that felt almost tangible. She reached out and gently placed a hand on my chest. The moment she touched me, it felt like a strong punch to my heart—a sudden jolt that sent waves of energy coursing through me. My breath caught in my throat, and I stumbled back, the world around me flickering as if reality itself was straining under the weight of her touch.

"Remember this feeling, Jack," she said softly, her voice resonating like a calming melody. "It is a reminder of life—the power of love, the strength of connection. You are not merely a passenger in your journey; you have the ability to change your fate."

But before I could respond, the mist began to swirl again, and the ethereal world of Mayari dissolved around me. I felt myself plummeting into darkness, a free fall that left my stomach churning. The air rushed past me, cold and biting, until suddenly, I was jolted awake once more.

I was no longer in the domain of Mayari; I was engulfed in chaos. Bright lights flashed before my closed eyes, accompanied by blaring sirens that pierced through the disorienting haze. I felt the hard surface beneath me, the slight tremor of movement, the frantic voices of paramedics echoing in the background.

"Get the defibrillator ready!" one voice shouted urgently.

The weight of my unconsciousness pressed heavily on me, but somewhere deep inside, I was aware of my surroundings—my mind fighting to resurface, grasping at the tendrils of consciousness. I could hear the sounds of an ambulance, the rhythmic beeping of machines, and the panicked shuffling of feet around me.

Suddenly, I was plunged back into darkness, and as I drifted, another voice broke through—a voice filled with anguish.

"Jack! Why did you have to pick her? Why couldn't you just stay at the bar with me?" It was Aeon, her tone tinged with desperation. "You should have known better than to leave us! Why does it always have to be Dina?"

"Why did you leave us?" she cried out, her voice breaking, carrying the weight of my absence. "You could have been here! We could have laughed, shared stories, made memories! But you chose to go home to her!"

Each word she uttered felt like a dagger to my heart, the betrayal of my own choices reverberating in my mind. I saw the vibrant scenes of that night flash before me—Aeon's laughter, her bright spirit lighting up the room, the way she always seemed to know how to lift my spirits when they faltered. She had been my confidante, my rock in so many ways. But now, all I could see was the heartbreak in her eyes, the fissures in our friendship that my decisions had created.

I could hear the hurt in her voice, a mixture of anger and sadness that cut deep. "I can't keep pretending everything is okay," she continued, her voice trembling. "It's not fair that she had you all those years while I stood on the sidelines, flirting and wishing it could have been me. I was right here, Jack, always ready to be the one you needed, yet you chose her."

As she spoke, I could feel the distance between us growing, a chasm created by my choices. I wanted to reach out, to mend what was broken, but the pain of my own decisions left me paralyzed. I could feel the tears in her eyes mirrored the tumult within me—confusion, regret, and a haunting sense of loss.

"Why couldn't you see me, Jack?" she implored, her voice a soft whisper now, laden with unspoken feelings. "I tried to be everything you needed, but you only had eyes for her. And now... now I'm left here alone, grappling with what we could have been."

Her anguish wrapped around me like a shroud, deepening the ache in my chest. I was trapped in this state, unable to provide comfort or answers, yet every fiber of my being screamed for her to understand—understand that I never meant for any of this to happen. I could only absorb her pain, wishing I could bridge the gap that had formed between us.

Again, I faded into darkness, only to be drawn back into the cacophony of sounds. I heard Jay muttering something under his breath, his voice barely audible over the noise. "I went through all that trouble and you'll just..." He sounded tired, almost indifferent. It barely registered at the time, just another offhand comment in the chaos.

As I hovered in this liminal space, the scene shifted again, and I was suddenly in a sterile hospital room, the air thick with antiseptic. My body lay motionless in a hospital bed, the steady beep of machines providing a rhythm to the unnerving silence. I was aware of everything but unable to respond.

I could hear her—Dina—her voice a desperate whisper that cut through the haze. "Jack, please," she said, her tone breaking, the anguish palpable in the air. "You have to come back to me. I can't... I can't do this without you." Her words were laced with desperation, echoing through the hollow space of my consciousness.

"I need you, Jack. You promised me you'd always be there. We were going to make so many more memories together... to see the world and make it ours. Don't leave me like this." The weight of her emotion filled the room, striking me like a physical blow. I felt the tears in my own eyes, even if I couldn't express them. I wanted so desperately to reach out to her, to tell her I was still here, that I wasn't going anywhere.

"You're my everything, Jack. Please, fight for us. Come back!" The rawness of her emotion cut through the chaos, a lifeline in the overwhelming darkness.

With each heartfelt plea, I could feel the tether that bound us, the love that connected our souls even in this fractured state. Her strength ignited a spark of hope deep within me.

Suddenly, I was jolted awake again. Mayari's presence was beside me, grounding me, and I could feel the energy she had gifted me surging through my body. I felt the familiar warmth of her love, the depth of our shared moments, pulling me back into the light.

"Dina," I whispered, though I knew she couldn't hear me. But I felt the pull of my heart, the commitment to return and fight for the life we had built together.

I had to return—not just for me, but for her.

"Dina..." The name echoed in my mind like a mantra, a lifeline in the swirling chaos. "Dina... Dina..." Each repetition became a plea, a desperate invocation of the love that had always guided me.

The weight of my decision settled heavily in my chest, yet with every utterance of her name, a flicker of strength ignited within me. The memories of her laughter, her warmth, the way her eyes sparkled when she spoke about the future we had dreamed of together—these images flooded my consciousness, pushing back the shadows that threatened to consume me.

"Dina," I whispered, my voice barely breaking through the fog. "Please... I'm coming back."

I felt a stirring in the air around me, as if my words reached beyond the confines of this ethereal space. A warmth enveloped me, wrapping around my heart, pulling me toward the light.

"Dina..." I repeated, louder now, my voice growing in confidence, each syllable resonating with the power of my love for her. "Dina! I need you! I'm fighting for us!"

As if my plea had transcended the boundaries of reality, I felt a response—a gentle tug at my soul, a connection stronger than anything I had ever known. "Jack..." A voice, soft and sweet, floated through the haze, breaking through the darkness. It was her, the sound of my name wrapped in the warmth of her love.

"Dina!" I called out, my heart racing. I could feel her presence, like a beacon guiding me home.

"I'm here, Jack," she whispered, and at that moment, I knew she was listening. My heart swelled with determination, and the path before me began to shimmer, guiding me toward her.

With every fiber of my being, I clung to the connection we shared, the love that had always been our anchor. I thought of all the moments we had shared, the dreams we had built together, and the life I yearned to reclaim.

"Dina... I'm coming back to you!" I cried out, my voice breaking free from the depths of despair.

The world around me began to pulse with energy, the colors blending and swirling, transforming into a vivid tapestry of memories and hopes. I felt a surge of power coursing through me, the essence of our love igniting a fire within my soul.

As I embraced the light, I could feel the barriers dissolving, the distance between us collapsing. My heart raced as I pushed through the darkness, propelled by the unbreakable bond we shared.

"Dina!" I shouted once more, the name reverberating through the ether, a declaration of my unwavering resolve.

And just like that, I felt myself being pulled back, the ethereal realm fading away, leaving only the warmth of her presence, a glowing light in the vast expanse of my heart.

But before I could fully return, a soft, melodic voice floated through the haze, reverberating like a gentle breeze. "Jack." It was Mayari, her ethereal form shimmering in the twilight. Her eyes sparkled with a wisdom that transcended time and space.

"You have made your choice," she said, her tone both soothing and firm. "But remember, with this new life comes the weight of your decisions."

I nodded, feeling the gravity of her words sink in. "I understand," I replied, my heart racing. "I won't take this for granted."

Mayari's gaze softened, and I sensed the warmth of her understanding. "You will be granted the chance to rewrite your story. Use it wisely. The past may be gone, but the lessons it taught you remain."

A shimmer of light danced around her, illuminating the space between us. "Love is a gift, Jack. Cherish it, nurture it. And remember, sacrifices come with a price. You must learn to balance your desires with the responsibilities of your heart."

"I will," I promised, a renewed sense of purpose flooding my veins. "I'll make every moment count."

With a gentle nod, Mayari began to fade, her presence like a whisper in the wind. "Then go, Jack. Embrace your new beginning, and never forget what truly matters."

As her essence dissipated into the light, I felt a surge of hope fill my being. "I'm coming back," I whispered, a sense of clarity washing over me.

Suddenly, the warmth enveloped me completely, and I felt my consciousness sharpen. The familiar beeping of machines, the sterile scent of antiseptic, and the bright overhead lights flooded my senses. I was awake. I was alive.

"Dina," I gasped, the reality of my surroundings settling in. I had returned—not just to the world, but to her.

Chapter 5

The sterile smell of antiseptic and the constant beeping of machines filled the air, creating an ambiance that was both foreign and strangely familiar. I blinked against the harsh hospital light, squinting as I adjusted to the reality of my surroundings. Each day blurred into the next, punctuated only by the soft creaking of the nurses' shoes and the flutter of medical charts being flipped open and shut.

"Jack," a warm voice broke through my fog. I turned my head, and there she was—Dina, my rock. Her presence was the only comfort amidst the chaos. Every day, she was there, her smile a beacon in this bleak place. "Good morning," I managed, my voice still hoarse from disuse. I could feel the weight of the past few weeks pressing down on me, but seeing her lightened that load, if only a little. "Morning! How are you feeling today?" she asked, her eyes searching mine for answers. "Like I've been run over by a truck," I said, forcing a chuckle, though I didn't really feel like laughing.

The heavy tinnitus still throbbed in my ears, a constant reminder of my injuries. "Doc says it'll fade. Just... no loud music for no w." "Guess you'll have to wait a bit longer for that concert, huh?" Dina smiled, but I could see the worry behind her eyes. "Yeah, but what's the rush? I just want to get through today," I replied, shifting slightly in my bed. The movement sent a jolt of pain through my body, a reminder of the fragility of my current state.

Dina pulled up a chair and settled beside me. "I'm here for all the days, Jack. Just focus on healing." Her words were like a soothing balm, wrapping around me. Each day, we created a routine. Mornings were filled with small exercises the nurses insisted I do to regain my strength. They were difficult, and I often grumbled about them, but Dina never let me skip a session. "Let's go for a walk," she said one day, her voice a gentle coaxing.

With her help, I swung my legs over the side of the bed, the coldness of the floor biting at my feet. As I stood, my knees felt wobbly, but I took a breath and pushed through. "Okay, one step at a time, right?" "Right," she encouraged, her hand steadying my elbow. We made our way down the corridor, the stark white walls lining our path. I could feel the stares of other patients and visitors, their eyes heavy with pity, but Dina's presence shielded me from it. "Look, it's not so bad," she said, pointing out a family gathered around a bouquet of flowers.

"See? Life goes on outside these walls." I nodded, though I struggled to grasp that concept. Life felt so distant from my little bubble of pain and recovery. I tried to focus on the little victories, like walking without the aid of a nurse, or being able to sit up without assistance. Days turned into weeks. The nurses began to recognize my face, and I memorized their names—Emily, Raj, Linda—their kindness became part of my daily rhythm.

They cheered me on as I improved, but it was Dina who pushed me to dig deeper. Every evening, after the sun dipped below the horizon and the hospital dimmed to a soft glow, we would sit together. Sometimes, we'd talk about trivial things—what show to binge next, or what we missed most about the outside world. Other times, we'd sit in silence, and I'd watch her as she flipped through a magazine, her brow furrowing at the articles."You know," she said one night, breaking the comfortable silence, "I've been thinking about your recovery.

You've come so far already.""Thanks to you," I replied, my voice barely above a whisper. "I don't know how I'd manage without you."Her cheeks flushed slightly, and she looked down. "We're in this together, Jack. Always."Six months dragged on, a test of patience and resilience. Each day was a battle, but with Dina by my side, I felt stronger. I cherished every moment with her, the small laughter we shared over silly hospital food, or the way her hand fit perfectly in mine.Finally, the day came when the doctor entered my room with a smile, clipboard in hand.

"Jack, I think it's time we talk about your discharge."The news hit me like a jolt of electricity. "Really? You mean I can go home?""Absolutely. You've made remarkable progress. Just a few more instructions, and you're free to go."I turned to Dina, her eyes sparkling with joy. "We did it," she whispered, tears brimming in her eyes." Yes, we did," I echoed, feeling a swell of hope. It wasn't just about leaving the hospital; it was about reclaiming my life.

As I packed my things, I felt a mix of anxiety and excitement. The world outside these walls felt both thrilling and intimidating. But I knew with Dina beside me, I was ready to face whatever came next.The moment I stepped out of the hospital, the sunlight washed over me like a warm embrace, dispelling the shadows that had clung to me for months. Dina squeezed my hand, her presence grounding me as we made our way to the car. "Are you ready for this?" she asked, her eyes sparkling with anticipation.

"Honestly? No idea what to expect," I admitted. "But I trust you." "Then let's go celebrate!" she said, her enthusiasm infectious. When we arrived at the park, I spotted Aeon and Jay setting up a picnic. A vibrant blanket was sprawled out under a tree, adorned with a spread of food that made my stomach growl. Jay waved at us, his trademark goofy grin plastered across his face.

Aeon stood next to him, arms crossed and lips pursed, her expression a mix of happiness and something else—maybe envy? "Hey, look who finally decided to join us!" Jay called out, his voice filled with cheerfulness. "Yeah, thanks for the invite, but what took you so long?" Aeon's tone was slightly sharp but playful. Dina and I approached, and I caught a glimpse of Aeon's eyes narrowing slightly as she saw our joined hands.

"I thought this was supposed to be a celebration," I said, trying to lighten the mood. "Of course! Just happy you're out of that hospital," Jay said, slapping me on the back. "We couldn't let you sit around and mope. We've got a whole day planned." Dina and I exchanged a glance, both sensing the subtle tension in the air. I settled onto the blanket, and Dina sat beside me, our fingers intertwined. As we dug into the food, I couldn't shake the feeling that Aeon was still holding something back. After a while, I decided to address it.

"Hey, Aeon," I said, casually picking at a sandwich. "You never came to visit me in the hospital. What was up with that?" Her expression faltered, a flicker of embarrassment crossing her features. "I was busy, Jack. Someone had to take care of your workload," she replied, her tone softening a bit. "Busy? Doing my workload?" I raised an eyebrow. "But Jay can come and go as he pleases? That feels a bit unfair."Jay shrugged, taking a large bite of his sandwich.

"I mean, I just showed up. Didn't really think much about it."Aeon shot him a teasing glare. "You're not exactly the poster child for responsibility, Jay. You'd probably mess it up if you cared."The mood shifted slightly, and I could feel Dina's hand squeeze mine tighter. "So, what? You thought I'd be better off alone?" I pressed gently, my curiosity piqued.

"You didn't even check in on me once.""Look, it's not like that," Aeon said, her voice softening. "I had a lot on my plate. I just didn't want to drag you down further.""Drag me down?" I replied, trying to keep it light. "You think I would have been upset to see a friend? I was stuck in that room for months, and I would have appreciated any company."Aeon sighed, her shoulders relaxing a bit.

"I get it. Maybe I should have tried harder. I just didn't want to bother you while you were recovering.""Bother me? Come on, Aeon. I had nothing but time," I said, my tone warm but firm. "It would have meant a lot to see you there."Aeon nodded, her expression softening. "I'm sorry, Jack. I really am. I just didn't know how to deal with it. You being hurt... it affected me more than I thought."I smiled, hoping to ease the tension. "Just promise me next time, if something's up, just talk to me. I'd hate to miss out on our friendship over something like this."Aeon managed a small smile back, her tension easing.

"Okay, deal."The conversation drifted back to lighter topics, filled with laughter and playful banter. As the sun dipped lower in the sky, I felt a sense of normalcy wash over me.The afternoon wore on, our energy fueled by food and the comfort of each other's company. But beneath it all, I could sense the undercurrents of unresolved feelings. Aeon's envy lingered in the air, her glances toward Dina revealing a mix of emotions.

Eventually, we sprawled on the blanket, the sun casting long shadows across the grass. I caught Aeon looking at us again, and a thought crossed my mind: Did she feel left out? I couldn't shake the feeling that her dynamic with Dina had shifted, and I hoped it wouldn't affect our friendship. Then, out of nowhere, Aeon smiled and said, "I have a little something for you, Jack."

She reached behind her and pulled out a guitar, its polished surface glinting in the afternoon light. "A recovery gift." Dina's expression faltered for a moment, a flicker of jealousy crossing her features before she masked it with a smile. I could see the mix of emotions in her eyes—happy for me, yet slightly uncomfortable with the gesture. "Wow, Aeon! This is amazing," I said, genuinely touched. I took the guitar from her, feeling the weight of it in my hands.

Memories of strumming chords and singing with friends flooded back to me. "Thank you." Aeon beamed at me, and in that moment, I felt a surge of warmth. I couldn't help but pull her into a hug. "This means a lot," I whispered, feeling her excitement radiate through me. It was clear she still had feelings for me, and that realization made me hesitate. But right now, I just wanted to enjoy this moment of gratitude. "Alright, rock star! Let's see if you still have it in you!" Jay chimed in, breaking the tension and shifting the focus. His voice was playful, but there was an underlying encouragement that pushed me forward.

Chapter 6

I chuckled, trying to shake off any lingering awkwardness. "I don't know if I can still play like I used to." I had spent so much time in the hospital that it felt like a lifetime since I'd strummed a single note. But I wanted to give it a shot."Come on, Jack. Just play something simple! You've got this!"Jay urged, practically bouncing with excitement.Taking a deep breath, I cradled the guitar, still feeling a little rusty.

I decided to play a slowed-down, ballad version of "Gusto Ko Lamang Sa Buhay." As I began to strum, my fingers felt clumsy, but I focused on the melody, pouring my heart into each note.The words flowed from my lips, and as I sang, I looked up to see Dina and Aeon, their faces lit with awe. They were lost in the moment, their eyes wide and fixed on me. I had never seen them look so captivated, almost as if the world around us faded away. It was a strange feeling, seeing them so mesmerized by my music, and it added a layer of confusion to my performance.As I reached the end of the song, I hesitated, unsure if it had been good or simply a jumble of sounds.

"Was it that bad?" I asked, furrowing my brow.Aeon, lost in her own thoughts, stepped forward and hugged me tightly, her embrace warm and lingering. For a moment, everything felt perfect.

But just as quickly, she broke the hug, her expression shifting as she caught the sharp look Dina shot her way. I felt a tension in the air, thick and undeniable."WTF was that song, man? That was something!" Jay exclaimed, his voice breaking the awkward silence.

I blinked, still trying to process what had just happened. "I just toned it down since I can't still play fast, but it's still 'Gusto Ko Lamang Sa Buhay.'"Jay raised an eyebrow, confusion etched across his face."From what band? Never heard of that song."Come on, Jay, Itchyworms!" I replied, exasperation creeping into my voice. "Why would I mess with you about that? This isn't a joke. We've been covering their songs since our college gigs!"Jay scratched his head, his confusion palpable."Dude, I swear I've never heard of them. Are you making this up? Is this some kind of inside joke?""Stop making jokes!" I snapped, my heart racing.

"This isn't funny. You really don't know who they are?""Maybe we're in some alternate universe where Itchyworms never existed? Like, how weird would that be?" Jay chuckled nervously, trying to lighten the mood.The laughter felt like a punch to the gut. I couldn't shake the feeling that something was off."This isn't some sick joke, Jay! They've been around forever. You can't tell me you haven't heard their songs!""Seriously, Jack," Dina chimed in, her brows knitted in confusion."I don't remember you ever mentioning them before.Are you sure they even exist?"I felt the weight of their disbelief settle in. A sickening knot formed in my stomach. "You're all kidding me, right?"

I reached into my pocket, pulling out my phone. I started typing, searching for Itchyworms.As I scrolled through the screen, my heart sank further. There was nothing. No articles, no songs, no albums. It was as if they had never existed. The weight of that real-ization pressed heavily on my chest, and I could feel the frustration boiling over."What the hell? This can't be right!" I exclaimed, my voice trembling with disbelief. "They're one of the biggest bands in the Philippines! They have classics, anthems—we used to play their stuff all the time!"Jay leaned back, crossing his arms.

"Maybe it's time you face the music, Jack. If no one remembers them, maybe they really are... gone."My mind raced. I wanted to scream, to argue, but instead, I felt a strange sense of dread wash over me. "You guys are really messing with me, huh? I don't like this joke you're playing."Aeon glanced between us, a hint of concern in her eyes. "Jack, we're not trying to upset you. We're just... confused."I shook my head, unable to articulate the whirlwind of thoughts racing through my mind.

"You know what? I need a minute." I stood up, needing space to breathe, to think, and to process everything. The vibrant picnic suddenly felt stifling, the laughter and sunlight closing in around me.As I walked away from the blanket, the sun dipped below the horizon, casting a warm glow that quickly faded into the cold grip of night. My phone buzzed in my pocket, and I ignored it. It was probably Dina, worried about me. I didn't want to talk to anyone right now.

I needed to be alone with my thoughts.Dark clouds gathered above me, and soon, the first drops of rain began to fall, turning into a steady downpour. I quickened my pace, seeking shelter under a nearby tree, but the chill seeped into my bones. As the rain drummed against the leaves, I felt a strange clarity amid the chaos of my mind.Then, like a bolt of lightning, the memory hit me: the deal I had made with Mayari after I crashed into the truck. She had given me a second chance at life.

But what if this was the cost? What if I had traded my life for the existence of Itchyworms? The thought twisted in my gut, a mix of dread and confusion. My heart raced as I pieced it together. The thought of never hearing their songs again, of a world that didn't know their music, was suffocating. I leaned against the tree, rain soaking through my clothes, feeling both angry and devastated. The laughter of my friends felt like a distant memory, replaced by a haunting silence. "What have I done?" I whispered to myself, the weight of the realization crashing down like the rain around me. My phone rang again, and this time, I glanced at the screen. It was Dina.

I hesitated, caught between wanting to pick up and needing to process everything swirling in my mind. But as I looked up at the dark sky, I could only think of the light that had been extinguished—my beloved band, my music, the essence of who I was. I couldn't answer her right now. As the rain poured harder, I closed my eyes and let the storm wash over me, hoping it would cleanse the bitterness of this impossible situation. But deep down, I knew that no amount of rain could wash away the weight of the decision I'd made.

I was alive, yes, but at what cost? At that moment, I heard footsteps approaching. I opened my eyes to see Aeon standing beneath the tree, holding an umbrella over her head. She said nothing, and I appreciated the silence. We stood there, two figures cloaked in the sound of the rain, each lost in our own thoughts. Finally, I broke the quiet. "Do you really not know the Itchyworms?" I asked, my voice calm, though my heart raced. She shook her head, a hint of confusion crossing her features. "No, I don't. I'm sorry. Should I?"I sighed, feeling a strange mix of disappointment and relief. "The song you just sang... it was beautiful," she said, a playful smile creeping onto her lips."Was it meant for me?"I stayed quiet, feeling the weight of her gaze.

The rain continued to fall, creating a rhythm that matched the tumult inside me.Then my phone rang again, and the sound pierced the air, pulling me back to reality. I glanced at the screen. It was Dina. I took a deep breath, pushing aside my swirling thoug hts."Hey, Dina," I said when I picked up, forcing a calmness into my voice."I'm heading home.""Jack! Where are you?"Her voice crackled through the line, tinged with concern."I'm okay," I reassured her. "I just need some time. I'll see you soon." I hung up and turned to Aeon, who was still holding the umbrella, the rain cascading around us."Thanks," I said simply, feeling the weight of our earlier conversation lingering in the air.

Without another word, I stepped away from the shelter of the tree and made my way into the rain, leaving her behind.As I stepped into the house, the familiar scent of home wrapped around me like a warm blanket, but I couldn't shake off the storm brewing in my mind. Dina was in the living room, but I didn't say anything as I passed her, my heart heavy with the weight of my thoughts. I needed space to process everything.I went straight ahead, finding solace in the stillness of our bedroom. The quiet felt deafening as I sat on the edge of the bed, contemplating the deal I had made with Mayari.

It gnawed at me, the realization that something—someone—im-portant might not exist anymore.Time slipped by. Dina rolled into the room, her wheelchair navigating the stairs with careful precision. I could feel her concern as she paused in the doorway, her caring eyes studying me. "Are you okay?" she asked softly. "Getting better," I replied, but I could feel the heaviness in my chest. "But what should I do?" "Regarding...?" she prompted, taking a step closer. "Regarding the fact that I know—or at least I think I know—something isn't existing in this world, and it's eating me up inside." My voice broke slightly, the weight of the admission feeling both liberating and crushing.

Dina furrowed her brow, her expression shifting as if a light bulb had gone off in her head. "What if it doesn't exist? Why not make it exist?" she said, her tone growing animated. I blinked at her, confused. "What do you mean?" "Jack, you're the only person who knows that band exists," she continued, her eyes sparkling with excitement. "Why not be the band itself? You can recreate the songs in your memory! You can bring them back to life!" The idea hung in the air, surreal yet exhilarating. Suddenly, a wave of happiness washed over me.

It was like a dam had broken within, and I could feel a rush of creativity surging forth. I could be the vessel for Itchyworms, channeling their music through me. "Dina, that's... that's brilliant!" I exclaimed, my mind racing with possibilities. "I could write new songs, bring back their spirit! We could do this together!" She smiled, a radiant light illuminating her face, and in that moment, I felt the darkness within me lifting. "You're not just alive, Jack. You're a creator. You have the power to make this real." I couldn't help but chuckle, the joy bubbling up uncontrollably. "So, what you're saying is, I should start my own band? Itchyworms 2.0?"

"Exactly!" she laughed, her laughter echoing in the room, filling the space with warmth. In that moment, everything felt right. I leaned in closer, feeling the magnetic pull between us. Our eyes locked, and without saying another word, we found ourselves wrapped in each other's arms, the world outside fading into not hingness.As the night deepened, our laughter softened into whispers, and those whispers ignited a spark of connection between us. In the quiet of our home, we lost ourselves in each other, the weight of the world fading away as we embraced.

With Dina by my side, I felt a renewed sense of purpose surging through me. I was ready to reclaim what was lost and give life back to Itchyworms through the music that flowed in my veins. As we held each other close, the warmth between us promised new beginnings and the creation of something beautiful—something that would resonate with the world, no matter the obstacles we faced.In that moment, I knew that together, we could bring the essence of my past into the present. I was alive, I was loved, and I was ready to make music again.

Chapter 7

The soft morning light filtered through the blinds as I squinted at the empty sticky notes scattered across my desk. I adjusted my new reading glasses—frames slightly too large for my face, but they were a reminder of how things had changed since my accident. My fingers hovered over a pen, tapping it lightly against my chin as I tried to conjure the elusive lyrics that had once flowed effortlessly from my mind.I took a deep breath and hummed the melody that danced at the edge of my consciousness. The notes felt familiar yet frustratingly out of reach. I squeezed my eyes shut, trying to focus on the sound, to pull the fragments from the shadows.

It was maddening, sitting there with nothing but the faintest echoes of songs I should know by heart."Hey, Jack, you okay?" Aeon's voice broke through my concentration, pulling me back to reality. She leaned against the doorframe, her arms crossed, eyebrows raised in that playful way that made it hard to stay serious."Yeah, I'm fine," I said, forcing a smile. "Just... trying to remember something."

Aeon stepped closer, glancing at the scattered notes. "Looks like you're planning a heist or something," she joked. "What's with all the blank sticky notes?"I chuckled, even though there was a lump in my throat. "Just trying to get my thoughts in order. It's... harder than it used to be." I wished I could tell her the truth—that I was desperately trying to remember lyrics from songs that no longer existed. But how could I explain that without sounding insane?"Must be some serious thoughts," Aeon said, picking up one of the notes and pretending to read it. "Let's see... 'blah, blah, blah, very deep and meaningful.'"I laughed, genuinely this time. "Pretty much."

"Maybe take a break? Clear your head?" She suggested. "Over-thinking can be a killer.""I'll try that," I said, knowing full well that I wouldn't. As Aeon walked away, I turned back to my desk, staring at the sticky notes like they might suddenly fill themselves in with the words I was so desperate to recall.Work was a distraction, but not enough of one. I found myself scribbling words and phrases on notepads between tasks, my mind drifting away from the spread-sheet on my computer screen. Every now and then, a melody would play in my head, and I'd freeze, trying to catch the fleeting notes before they slipped away.

During lunch, I sat alone in the office pantry, half-listening to the hum of the microwave, the chatter of my colleagues, and the faint rhythm tapping in my brain. I knew the melody. It was right there, like a word on the tip of my tongue, but when I tried to hum it out, the tune twisted into something unrecognizable."Hey, Earth to Jack," Jay said, sliding into the seat across from me. He was grinning, but there was a sharpness to his eyes that I couldn't quite place.

"You look like you're trying to solve the meaning of life over there."I blinked, shaking off the fog. "Just... lost in thought."Jay leaned back, eyeing me curiously. "Must be some heavy thoughts.

You've been pretty spaced out lately. What's going on?" I hesitated. I couldn't tell him about the songs, about how they were slipping away. Jay wouldn't understand—how could he, when no one but me even knew they existed? "Just trying to remember something, that's all.

"Jay shrugged, his grin widening. "Well, don't let it drive you crazy. If it's that important, it'll come back to you." He gave me a playful nudge. "And if not, you've still got us to keep you grounded." Back at my desk, I tried to work, but my mind kept drifting. I pulled out a sticky note, jotting down random words that felt like they were part of something bigger, something that used to make sense: "sampaguita," "beer," "over the moon." Each word was like a tiny piece of a jigsaw puzzle, but I didn't have the picture on the box to guide me. I glanced at the clock. It was only mid-afternoon, but it felt like I'd been here for days. I needed to get out, to clear my head, like Aeon had suggested.

So, I grabbed my things and headed out, hoping that maybe the walk would help, that maybe something in the city would jog my memory. As I stepped outside, the sun hit my face, and I found myself humming again, the melody almost clear this time. I closed my eyes, trying to hold on to it, trying to keep it from slipping away like smoke. But no matter how hard I tried, the words remained just out of reach, like a dream I could barely remember upon waking. I wandered through the city aimlessly, humming under my breath, hoping that the sounds of the streets, the buzz of the crowd, might unlock whatever was buried in my head.

But all I had were fragments, like broken shards of glass that didn't fit together anymore. My feet took me past shops, cafes, and street vendors, my mind barely registering them as I tried to focus on the melody that had been haunting me all day. Then, almost by accident, it happened. A phrase, a rhythm. It slipped out of my mouth before I could even catch it, the same song I had sung at the picnic. The one that had made everyone stop and listen, though none of them could quite grasp why it felt so familiar. I stood still, letting the words come, my voice steady but low, as if afraid that if I sang too loud, I'd lose it again.

The melody was there, the lyrics flowing through me as if I'd known them all along. For a brief, perfect moment, it felt like I had recaptured a piece of myself that I thought was gone. "Hey." The voice was smooth, dripping with a kind of cool confidence that immediately made me wary. I turned, and there she was—dressed in a sleek, tailored outfit that hugged her curves just right, lips painted a shade of red that could kill, a hint of a smirk on her face. "You've got a terrible voice," she said, her words like silk dipped in acid, eyes glinting as they sized me up. "But that song… it's got something, doesn't it? The melody, the lyrics… yeah, there's a spark there." I didn't know how to respond.

She was looking at me like I was a puzzle she was itching to solve, or maybe a deal she was already halfway through closing. It made me uneasy. "It's nothing," I mumbled, shoving my hands into my pockets. "Just something I was trying to remember." She tilted her head slightly, her smile widening with a predatory edge. "Nothing? Sweetheart, I don't do 'nothing.' I'm Angga. I spot talent, or potential, when I see it. And this—" she gestured vaguely toward me, as if trying to capture whatever it was she saw—"this could be something big. But not with you mumbling it like that." My stomach twisted. "I'm not interested." Her smile didn't falter; it only sharpened. "Not yet," she said, her voice low and smooth, like a promise and a threat all at once. "But you will be. Trust me on that. I have a way of turning little nothings into big somethings. And right now, you're sitting on a goldmine, whether you realize it or not."

I felt a chill creep down my spine at her words. It was as if she saw straight through me, stripping away my uncertainty and exposing a raw potential I wasn't even sure existed. "Goldmine?" I echoed, skepticism lacing my tone. "I'm just some guy who can't even remember the lyrics to a song." Angga stepped closer, the scent of her perfume—a heady mix of jasmine and something sharper—filling the air between us. "That's where you're wrong, Jack," she said, her voice now a conspiratorial whisper. "You have something that can't be taught or bought. It's instinctive. The way you sang, even just now... it resonated. People want to feel something, and you have the ability to make them feel. You just need a little guidance."

I raised an eyebrow, trying to maintain a façade of indifference despite the flutter of interest in my chest. "And what's in it for you? Why would you want to help me?" She laughed softly, a sound both melodic and dangerous. "It's simple. I see potential, and I know how to harness it. I've got connections, resources. I can turn that 'something' into a career. But make no mistake; I don't do charity. If you shine, I shine. It's a win-win." I hesitated, weighing her words. "And what do you expect from me? Just to sing a song?"

"Not just any song," she replied, her expression serious now. "You need to find the heart of your music, the essence of what you want to express. It's not enough to mumble out lyrics. You need to own it. And that takes time, effort, and, of course, a little investment." "What kind of investment?" I asked, wary. Her smile returned, but this time it felt like a blade concealed behind her lips. "I'll help you with the craft, refine your sound, get you noticed. But you'll need to be all in. This is about commitment, Jack. I don't work with half-measures.""I'm not sure I can do this alone," I admitted, the doubt creeping back in.

"But I know people who can help. My former bandmate Jay is a fantastic drummer, and Aeon has an incredible voice. They could bring the sound to life, but they're not exactly in the music scene anymore."Angga's eyes lit up at the mention of my friends. "Now we're talking. Surrounding yourself with talent can only help you, especially if you've got people who believe in your vision. If you think they'll jump on board, I'm all in for a group effort.""Would you really help us?" I asked, surprised by how easy she made it sound."Absolutely," she said, leaning back with confidence.

"But you'll need to convince them first. Bring them in, show them what you're working with. I want to see you all create something that makes people sit up and take notice. That song you sang earlier—there's potential in it. Let's build on that."I felt a mix of relief and excitement."Alright, I'll reach out to them. But you'll have to understand—they might not be interested in jumping back into the spotlight."Angga waved her hand dismissively. "That's where my charm comes in. I can be persuasive when I need to be. Just focus on your part. I'll handle the rest."

Chapter 8

As I contemplated the prospect of bringing my friends back into my life—and into a new project—I could feel the flutter of anticipation growing in my chest. The thought of reuniting with Jay and Aeon, rekindling that spark of creativity we once shared, was intoxicating. "Okay," I said, feeling more resolute. "Let's do this." "Great!" Angga said, her smile wide and genuine now. "Get your band together, and we'll set up a meeting. I want to see what you all can create." As we sealed the deal with a firm handshake, I could sense the shift in the air, a surge of excitement that hinted at a new beginning.

Maybe, just maybe, I was finally on the path to reclaiming my lost melody—not just for myself, but for my friends as well. I sat at my desk, staring at the sticky notes littering the surface, each one holding a half-formed lyric or melody I was desperate to remember. The office buzzed around me, a symphony of typing and muted conversations, but all I could think about was the idea brewing in my mind. I glanced over at Aeon, who was at her desk, her fingers flying over her keyboard. She had this infectious energy that always made the day a little brighter. Jay was nearby, chatting with another coworker, his laid-back demeanor a stark contrast to my growing anxiety."Hey, Aeon! Jay!" I called out, summoning their attention.

They both turned toward me, curiosity etched on their faces." Yeah, Jack?" Aeon replied, her smile inviting."Can you guys come to the coffee shop with me after work? I need to talk to you about something important."Jay leaned back in his chair, raising an eyebrow."Important? This sounds serious. Are you okay?"I nodded, trying to keep my composure. "Yeah, I'm fine. It's just… about music. I think we should revive our college band."Aeon's interest piqued instantly. "Our college band? Really? What brought this on?""Just some ideas I've been having," I said, feeling a mix of excitement and apprehension. "But I want to discuss it in a more relaxed setting. You know, the coffee shop atmosphere."Jay shrugged, grinning.

"Count me in. I could use a caffeine fix anyway.""Sounds good to me!" Aeon agreed, her eyes sparkling with enthusiasm. "What time are we meeting?""Let's say around six?" I suggested relief washing over me."Perfect! I'll see you guys then," I said, a smile spreading across my face as they both nodded and turned back to their work.The hours dragged on, my anticipation growing as the clock ticked closer to six. I couldn't shake the feeling that this was a pivotal moment for all of us. I glanced at the sticky notes once more, gathering my thoughts and rehearsing what I would say.

Finally, the workday ended, and I found myself standing outside the coffee shop, the familiar scent of roasted beans filling the air. I leaned against the wall, breathing in the aroma, my mind racing with possibilities.When Aeon and Jay arrived, I pushed off the wall and waved them over."Thanks for coming, guys.""Of course! What's the big idea?" Jay asked, his casual demeanor making it easier to manage my nerves. I took a deep breath, ready to share my vision. "Let's grab some coffee first, and then I'll explain everything." As we settled into a cozy corner of the coffee shop, the comforting hum of chatter and the clinking of cups surrounded us.

I watched as Aeon and Jay sipped their drinks, their expressions curious and expectant. "Okay, so here's the deal," I began, leaning forward, my heart racing with excitement. "I met this producer today—Angga, her name is. She noticed the weight of the song I was humming earlier and said it had potential. She believes we could create something special." Aeon's eyes widened. "A producer? That's amazing! What did she say?" "She thinks there's something there, something worth exploring. But here's the catch," I said, holding up a finger to emphasize my point. "She wants me to lead the project. I'd be in charge of all the writing." Jay raised an eyebrow.

"You? Writing all the songs? How does that work?" "Exactly," I replied, my voice steadying. "That's where you guys come in. I want us to form the band again—revive our college band. I have ideas, and I remember fragments of songs that I want to develop. I just need your voices and creativity to bring them to life." "Wait, wait," Aeon interjected, her enthusiasm bubbling over. "Are you saying we'd be working with a producer? Like, for real? This could be huge!" "Exactly!" I said, feeding off her excitement. "But it's going to take all of us. I'll focus on the lyrics and melodies, but I need you two to help shape the sound. Jay, your drumming and Aeon, your vocals—together, we could make something incredible." Jay leaned back, considering my words. "It's a big step, Jack. What if it doesn't work out?"

"Then we try again," I replied, feeling a surge of determination. "But I believe in this. I believe in us. And honestly, this feels like the first real chance I've had since… well, everything that happened. We can create something that resonates, something that tells our stories."Aeon nodded, her excitement turning serious. "I'm in. I've missed making music, and if you're leading the way, I trust you."Jay shrugged, a playful grin creeping onto his face. "What the hell. Count me in, too. Let's see where this goes.""Awesome!"

I exclaimed, relief washing over me. "Let's do this, then. I'll start jotting down ideas, and we can meet regularly to work on everything together."As we clinked our cups together in a toast to our new venture, I felt a flicker of hope ignite within me. This was the start of something new, a chance to reclaim not just my memories but to create new ones with my friends.Jay suddenly leaned forward, a serious expression crossing his face. "So, does Dina know about this? I mean, you're diving into a pretty big project."I felt my stomach twist at the mention of her name.

"Uh, no… not yet," I admitted, scratching the back of my head. "I didn't run this by her first."Jay raised an eyebrow. "You might want to do that before we get too deep into it. You know how she is. If you spring this on her later, it might not go over so well.""Yeah, you're right," I said, a pang of guilt settling in. "Dina deserves to be in the loop. I should have thought about it. She's always been supportive of my music dreams, and I don't want to surprise her without talking it over first."Aeon leaned closer, a teasing smile playing on her lips.

"So, you're telling me you can dive headfirst into the music scene but you're afraid to talk to your wife about it? I didn't take you for the timid type, Jack."I chuckled, feeling the warmth of her gaze.

"Hey, I'm not timid. I just know how to pick my battles. And this one? It's worth approaching carefully."She laughed softly, her eyes sparkling. "I get it. Just don't forget to bring me along for the ride. You know I have a knack for turning ideas into something... spectacular."

"Spectacular, huh?" I smirked, leaning back in my chair. "You're not just a pretty face with a great voice; you're also a natural at hype. Maybe you should be my co-manager."Her expression turned playful as she leaned in, lowering her voice."Only if I get to pick the outfits. We can't have you dressing like a dad on stage."I feigned offense, placing a hand over my heart. "Hey! I'll have you know my style is top-notch."

"Sure, if you think those socks with sandals are making a state-ment," she shot back, a playful grin on her face. The easy banter felt like old times, a comforting warmth wrapping around us.Jay cleared his throat, trying to stifle a laugh. "As much as I enjoy this fashion critique, let's focus on the music. So, does Dina know about this?"I felt the warmth of Aeon's teasing linger, but Jay's question pulled me back to reality. "I'll talk to her," I said, a surge of determination rising within me. "I want her to be part of this journey, too, even if it's just as a sounding board for ideas.

She knows my heart better than anyone else."Jay and Aeon exchanged knowing glances. "Good call, Jack," Jay said, giving me a supportive nod. "Just be honest with her. She'll appreciate it .""Absolutely," I replied, feeling a sense of relief wash over me. "I'll make sure to have that conversation tonight. Thanks for the reminder."We spent the rest of our coffee break brainstorming names for our revived band and throwing around ideas for our first song, the excitement of the new venture washing over any lingering doubts.

But in the back of my mind, I knew the conversation with Dina would be the real challenge.As I walked through the door, the familiar scent of fried snacks and freshly brewed coffee enveloped me, a comforting reminder of home. The soft glow of the overhead lights illuminated our small sari-sari store, tucked neatly in the corner of our garage. I found Dina behind the counter, her hair tied back in a messy bun, her brow slightly furrowed with exhaustion from the day's work."Hey, love," I greeted her, my voice softer than usual. She looked up, offering a tired smile that barely reached her eyes."Hey, Jack. How was your day?" she asked, wiping her hands on a dish towel as she stepped away from the counter."It was good, but I need to talk to you about something important," I said, trying to gauge her mood.

She nodded, setting the towel aside and leaning against the counter, her arms crossed as she faced me.I took a deep breath, the words I had rehearsed in my mind suddenly feeling heavier than I expected. "I've been thinking a lot about what you said... about bringing Itchyworms' music to life. I want to pursue that idea, to form a band with Jay and Aeon."Dina's brow furrowed slightly, her exhaustion evident as she remained silent, listening intently.I continued, feeling a mix of excitement and nerves. "I met a producer today, Angga.

She's going to help us spread our music, the kind that I once believed in—music that could spark something in people, just like it did for me."Dina's eyes searched mine, her expression unreadable as she took in my words. "And... you really think this will work?" she finally asked, her voice soft but steady."I do," I replied, a surge of hope igniting within me. "I believe we can make something special. This is my chance to create again, to honor the music that once meant so much to me. I want to make you proud." Dina sighed, her shoulders relaxing slightly as she absorbed my enthusiasm.

"Jack, I've seen how passionate you are about music. But it's not just about creating—it's also about the time and effort it takes. Are you ready for that?" I nodded, determination coursing through me. "I am. I've thought about it a lot. I want to do this for us, for the music, and to keep that spirit alive. I want to share it with everyone, and I want you to be a part of it." For a moment, she stood quietly, her gaze drifting toward the shelves stocked with snacks and drinks. I could see the weight of her exhaustion mingling with a flicker of hope in her eyes. "Okay," she finally said, her voice barely above a whisper.

"I'll support you, but you need to promise me that you won't lose sight of what really matters—us." "I promise," I assured her, reaching across the counter to take her hands in mine. "You and our life together will always come first. This is just another piece of that life, another dream we can chase." She squeezed my hands, a small smile breaking through her fatigue. "Then let's make it happen, Jack. Just... don't forget to come home to me every night, okay?" I chuckled softly, feeling lighter. "You won't get rid of me that easily. I'm in this for the long haul." With a sense of shared understanding, we stood there for a moment, connected by our dreams and the challenges ahead.

The exhaustion of the day seemed to fade, replaced by a renewed sense of purpose as we faced the future together. In my mind, I couldn't help but remember our wedding day—a time when music filled our lives with hope and joy. Back then, we were young and full of dreams, my bandmates and I envisioning a future where our songs would resonate far and wide. But then the tragedy struck, leaving Dina in that wheelchair, and our dreams were buried beneath the weight of reality. That's why I quit the band and looked for a company to become an employee.

Now, more than ever, I was determined to rise from the ashes, to chase the fame we once dreamed of—not just for myself but to gather the money for her surgery. If I could create something beautiful again, maybe I could turn our shared dream into a reality.

Chapter 9

The dim light of our rehearsal space flickered as I set up my guitar, anticipation buzzing in the air. It felt surreal, declaring ourselves the new Itchyworms—a name I had cherished since childhood. Here we were: Jack S. Jaques, Aeon K. Lee, and Jay V. Erjon. A trio forged from our individual struggles, ready to carve our place in the music scene. As I adjusted the guitar strap, the weight of the moment brought me back to when it all began, years ago in college. I could almost see the old campus, the familiar faces of classmates, and the chaotic energy of youth that had brought us together. Back then, everything was different. Simpler, maybe. I was just a kid who loved music, not yet tangled in the complexities of life, love, and sacrifices.

It was my sophomore year, a typical humid afternoon, and the university courtyard was buzzing with activity. I'd just finished a long day of lectures and was on my way to grab a quick bite when I heard it—faint, muffled music seeping out from one of the old practice rooms. The melody was raw, a bit rough around the edges, but it had a charm that caught my ear. Curious, I followed the sound, pushing open the slightly ajar door. Inside, Aeon was seated at a keyboard, her fingers lightly pressing down on the keys, coaxing out a melody that seemed to hang in the air.

She was humming along, eyes closed, completely lost in the music. I hadn't seen her like that before—so relaxed, so in tune with what she was playing. We'd been in a few classes together, but I'd never really talked to her. She was always quiet, keeping to herself, but now I could see this other side of her, and it was… captivating."Hey, that sounds pretty good," I said, leaning against the doorway. Aeon startled a little, snapping out of her trance.

She looked up at me, and for a moment, I thought she might tell me to leave, but then she smiled, a bit shyly."Thanks… It's just something I've been working on," she replied, her voice soft but clear."I didn't think anyone would hear it.""Well, I did. And I liked it," I said, stepping inside. "I'm Jack, by the way. We're in Econ together, right?""Yeah, I know," she said, glancing down at the keys, as if suddenly self-conscious. "I'm Aeon."

"That's a cool name. You play really well."The conversation flowed from there, and soon we were talking about music—bands we loved, songs that made us feel things words couldn't. We ended up spending hours in that cramped room, exchanging stories about our favorite tracks, our guilty pleasures, and what made us want to play. By the end of it, I'd already decided: I wanted to play with her.Over the next few weeks, we started meeting up after classes, jamming together whenever we could. We weren't thinking about starting a band; we were just two people who liked making music. But then Jay showed up.

I snapped back to the present, the familiar feeling of my guitar against my chest grounding me. Jay was adjusting his Cajon, a focused look on his face. I couldn't help but smile, remembering how we'd met him, too. He'd been Aeon's friend from high school, a guy with a big personality and even bigger dreams.

"Jack, you have to meet Jay," Aeon had said one day, practically dragging me to a different part of campus. We rounded a corner, and there he was, banging out a beat on a set of old, mismatched drums someone had left behind in the courtyard. His rhythm was infectious, his hands moving so fast they were just a blur. I had no idea how Aeon convinced him to lug all that gear onto campus, but there he was, giving an impromptu show to a small crowd of curious onlookers. He looked up, noticed us, and broke into this huge grin. "Hey, Aeon! Who's your friend?" he called out, his voice loud and confident.

That was Jay—never afraid to make himself heard. "This is Jack. He plays guitar," she said, smiling as if she'd just completed a puzzle. "Oh yeah?" Jay's eyes lit up. "You any good?" "I guess you'll just have to find out," I said, matching his grin. And that was it. The three of us spent that afternoon jamming in the middle of campus, much to the amusement of everyone around. It was messy, chaotic, and completely unplanned—but it felt right. By the end of that day, we knew we had something special. We didn't have a name or any clear direction, but we had each other, and that was enough. Aeon, with her soft yet powerful melodies; Jay, with his unrelenting, infectious beats; and me, trying to stitch it all together with my guitar.

I returned to the present, my gaze shifting between Aeon and Jay, who were now setting up their instruments. So much had changed since those college days, but the core of it was still there—the same energy, the same drive. Aeon's fingers danced over the piano keys, testing out a few notes, while Jay's hands drummed a familiar rhythm on his Cajon, his eyes full of excitement. We were different people now, older and maybe a bit more jaded, but the music still brought us back to who we were, back when we didn't have a care in the world.

I adjusted my guitar strap, letting the strings ring out as I strummed a few chords.It felt surreal, declaring ourselves the new Itchyworms—a name I had cherished since childhood. Back then, I never imagined I'd be here, reclaiming that name and trying to bring it back to life. But it felt right, like the final piece of a puzzle that had been missing for years."Okay, guys, let's take it from the top," I said, my voice steady. Aeon nodded, her eyes meeting mine for a brief moment, and I saw a flicker of something—determination, maybe, or something deeper. Jay cracked his knuckles, his trademark smirk already in place."Let's make it count, huh?" Jay said, his tone playful but laced with a challenge. "This needs to be unforgettable."I couldn't help but agree.

This was our moment—a chance to resurrect the melodies that had shaped my dreams. For better or worse, we were going to do this, together.As we started playing the ballad version of "Gusto ko lamang sa buhay," the song that had captivated everyone when I first sang it at the picnic, the room filled with energy. My heart swelled with pride and nostalgia as we poured our souls into the music. Each note resonated with a passion I had felt for so long. Aeon's voice and piano playing captured a surreal emotion, weaving a tapestry of sound that enveloped us.

I could almost hear Dina cheering us on, her spirit lifting us through lyrics that spoke of dreams and desires.After a few takes, we finally hit a rhythm that felt just right. I glanced at Aeon, who was lost in the moment, fingers gliding across the keys like they were made for this. Jay kept the beat on his Cajon, and in that fleeting moment, everything aligned perfectly. It felt like magic."Now that was fire!" Jay exclaimed when we finished. His excitement ignited something in me, but I could sense a nagging urgency beneath it. "We need to film this—like, right now. Angga's gonna love it."My stomach twisted at the mention of Angga. The slick producer had offered us a deal that felt too good to be true, despite the unsettling aura she exuded. I knew we were flirting with danger, but the allure of fame was hard to resist, especially for someone like me who had sacrificed so much for love and dreams.

Dina entered, her wheelchair gliding gracefully behind her. Her radiant smile was like sunlight breaking through clouds. "Hey, can I film you guys?" she asked, her voice bright with enthusiasm."Of course!" I replied, a rush of gratitude filling me. "We need your magic behind the camera."As Dina set up her phone, a surge of determination coursed through me. This was for her—for us. I wanted to create something beautiful that could resonate beyond our little circle and reach out to touch lives."Ready? Three, two, one, go!" she called out, and we launched into the song again. This time, I poured every ounce of emotion into it, hoping the rawness would translate on camera.

Between notes, I caught glimpses of Dina's joy and pride reflected in her eyes, driving me to give even more.Once we finished, she excitedly reviewed the footage, her eyes sparkling. "I can't wait to post this! It's going to blow up!"And blow up it did. Days passed, and the video exploded across social media, surpassing even the current top videos. The combination of our heartfelt performance and Aeon's beauty—her pleasant voice that could charm anyone—captivated audiences everywhere."Look at this!" Jay shouted, holding up his phone. "We're trending! Can you believe it?"The song was quickly gaining traction. Comments flooded in, praising our talent and begging for more. I couldn't believe how fast it was happening. Our little practice session had turned into a sensation overnight, and I felt both exhilarated and terrified.

But amidst all this success, Angga lurked like a predator, ready to capitalize on our moment. I could almost feel her calculating gaze on us, plotting her next move. She reached out to us, her smooth words dripping with temptation. "This is just the beginning. Let's turn this into something monumental."The allure of fame was intoxicating, but I couldn't shake the feeling that we were dancing on the edge of a cliff, with Angga guiding our steps. Would we be able to keep our footing, or would we tumble into the depths of her manipulation?"Eyyyyyyyyy!"Jay called out, nudging my shoulder and laughing. "Let's get this video up and show the world what we've got!"With laughter and camaraderie enveloping us, I felt a shift inside me—a renewed purpose. We were starting to create something special, something that felt like it could change everything.

But in the back of my mind, the question lingered: at what cost?As the days rolled on, the whirlwind of our newfound popularity was both exhilarating and disorienting. The video had gone viral, amassing views at a staggering rate. My phone buzzed incessantly with notifications, a constant reminder of our rapid rise to fame. Each ping sent a thrill through me, but alongside it, a knot of anxiety tightened in my stomach. We began rehearsing more frequently, trying to ride the wave of our success. Each session was a blend of hope and uncertainty, the energy in the room pulsing with both ambition and underlying tension. Aeon, always a beacon of positivity, dove into her piano playing with even more passion, her voice soaring through the chords. Jay, ever the showman, was eager to keep the rhythm going on his Cajon, always pushing for that next level of excitement. But Angga's presence loomed larger with each passing day.

She had reached out to us, suggesting we meet to discuss the next steps for our "brand." I felt a mix of anticipation and dread. The prospect of working with her was tantalizing—she had the connections and influence we desperately needed—but the way she smiled, that predatory glint in her eyes, made me uneasy. One evening after practice, as the sun dipped below the horizon, painting the sky in hues of orange and purple, we gathered around a small table in a nearby café. Dina had insisted on joining us, her laughter lighting up the atmosphere as she encouraged us to celebrate our success. I glanced around the table—Aeon's smile was radiant, Jay was animatedly recounting our latest social media stats, and Dina looked proud yet contemplative.

"Can you believe this is happening?" Aeon said, her eyes sparkling with excitement. "We're making a name for ourselves!" "It's insane," Jay replied, his grin wide. "We need to capitalize on this momentum. Get some gigs, maybe even an album out!" I nodded, the thrill of their enthusiasm mixing with my unease. "We have to be careful, though. Angga wants to meet with us, and I'm not sure about her intentions." Dina's expression shifted, a hint of concern in her gaze. "Jack, just be cautious. Remember, not everyone has your best interests at heart. Don't let the excitement blind you."

Her words lingered in my mind, weaving through my thoughts as we continued discussing plans for our next steps. We couldn't ignore the fact that our rise was meteoric, but at what cost? Angga had already made it clear that she wanted to shape our image, to mold us into something that fit her vision. After we finished our drinks, Jay stood up, pumping his fist in the air. "Let's make this happen, guys! We're the Itchyworms, and we're just getting started!" As we walked back to the rehearsal space, I felt a renewed sense of determination. We had something special—something worth fighting for. But beneath that, a gnawing doubt remained. Would Angga's involvement alter what we had built?

Chapter 10

A few days later, we finally met with Angga. She chose a sleek, upscale restaurant, the kind that oozed opulence and exclusivity. As we sat at a table adorned with white linens and flickering candles, I felt out of place amidst the polished ambiance. Angga arrived, her presence commanding the room as she swept in, exuding confidence. "Jack, Aeon, Jay," she greeted us with a dazzling smile. "I've been following your journey, and I'm impressed. You have something unique here, and I want to help you take it to the next level." Her words felt like a double-edged sword. "What do you have in mind?" I asked cautiously, my heart racing. Angga leaned in, her voice low and persuasive.

"We can create a brand around you, develop a sound that resonates with the audience, and push for a record deal. You could be the next big thing in the industry. All I need is your trust and commitment." The allure of her offer hung in the air like sweet nectar. I could almost taste the success she was promising, but at the same time, a voice inside me whispered caution. What would it mean to surrender our creative control to someone like her? "I appreciate the offer," I replied, trying to keep my tone neutral. "But we want to stay true to our music, to ourselves." Angga's smile faltered for just a moment, but she quickly recovered.

"Of course, authenticity is key. But trust me, you'll need a strong strategy to navigate this industry. There are many players, and it can be cutthroat." As the meeting progressed, I watched my band-mates' reactions. Aeon seemed enchanted, hanging on Angga's every word, while Jay appeared more intrigued than cautious. I felt torn, like a ship caught in a storm. The potential for greatness lay ahead, but the price felt steep. After Angga left, I found myself staring out the window, lost in thought. "What do you guys think?" I finally asked, turning to Aeon and Jay. "Are we ready to make that leap?" "I think it's a fantastic opportunity," Aeon replied, her enthusiasm infectious.

"We can reach so many people, Jack. Imagine our music touching lives!" Jay nodded, his eyes gleaming with ambition. "We'd be foolish not to take her seriously. This could change everything for us." I felt the weight of their expectations pressing down on me. They were excited, ready to embrace this chance, but my gut churned with uncertainty. "Let's sleep on it," I suggested. "We can talk more tomorrow." That night, as I lay in bed, I couldn't escape the swarm of thoughts buzzing in my head. The euphoria of our sudden rise was intoxicating, but there was something unsettling about it too.

Sure, we had been propelled to fame by the virality of "Gusto ko lamang sa buhay," but a nagging question gnawed at me: Was our music really good enough? Or was it just a fluke, a lucky hit boosted by the charm of Aeon's beauty and the nostalgia of a ballad? Angga's words echoed in my mind—"We need to create a brand, develop a sound that resonates." Did that mean she wanted us to change, to mold ourselves into something that fit her modern, sleek idea of success? I rolled onto my side, staring at the faint light filtering through the curtains.

Do we need to change to stay relevant? I thought about the songs that shaped me, the raw, unpolished beauty of the Itchyworms' original sound. It wasn't about trends or chasing what was popular—it was about heart, about truth. That's what had drawn me to their music in the first place.But could that still resonate with a new generation?As I drifted into a restless sleep, I resolved that we needed to find out. We weren't just going to be puppets in Angga's game—we were going to prove ourselves, or fail trying.

The next morning, the sun was barely up when I found myself wide awake, a clear plan forming in my head. If Angga wanted us to fit into her mold, we'd have to show her why that wasn't necessary. We needed to prove that our sound, our way, was just as powerful and relevant as anything she could come up with.As we gathered in the rehearsal space, I could feel the anticipation humming between us.Jay was bouncing on his heels, tapping out rhythms on the edge of his Cajon, while Aeon was softly playing a melody, her fingers almost absentmindedly gliding over the keys."I've made a decision," I said, my voice cutting through the morning quiet.

Aeon and Jay turned to me, their expressions a mix of curiosity and concern."We're not going to let Angga dictate our sound," I continued. "But I also understand that she's right about one thing—if we're going to make it, we need to show we can still connect with the audience, even the younger crowd."Jay raised an eyebrow. "So what's the plan? We just say no to her deal?""No," I said, a grin tugging at my lips. "We challenge her."Aeon's eyes widened. "Challenge her? How?"I took a breath, letting my nerves settle.

"An on-the-spot song creation battle. We pit ourselves against one of her top artists. If we win, we keep our sound, and she supports us on our terms. If we lose, we go along with her vision."Jay let out a low whistle. "You're crazy, man. But I love it."Aeon looked thoughtful, her fingers still resting on the keys. "It's risky, but it could work. We'd get to show exactly why our sound matters."I nodded, feeling a swell of determination. "It's a gamble, but it's one I'm willing to take. We can't just let someone else decide who we are."

The meeting with Angga was tense, the kind of atmosphere where you could almost see the sparks crackling in the air. She listened to my proposal with an amused smile, her eyes narrowing slightly as she processed my words."So, you're challenging me," she said, her tone silky and condescending. "An on-the-spot song battle between your little band and one of my artists. Do you have any idea what you're asking for, Jack?""I do," I said, my voice steady. "If we lose, we'll do things your way. Change our sound, our image, everything. But if we win, we do it our way, and you support us without trying to change who we are."

Angga's lips curled into a smile, a flash of teeth that sent a shiver down my spine. "You're bold, I'll give you that. But I'll play along. Consider it a deal." She leaned back, her eyes gleaming with a mix of amusement and challenge. "But don't think for a second that I'm going to go easy on you. I'll bring my best, and you better be ready.""We will be," I said, meeting her gaze head-on. "Just name the time and place."Angga stood up, straightening her sleek jacket. "This weekend. I'll set it up at one of my studios. Bring your best, Jack. I'd hate to see you lose because you underestimated what it takes to make it in this industry."

As we left the meeting, I felt a rush of adrenaline, but also a gnawing sense of fear. We were going to be stepping into Angga's territory, playing by her rules. But this was our shot—our chance to prove that we didn't need to compromise who we were to make it.Over the next few days, we practiced relentlessly. Every moment we weren't rehearsing, we were brainstorming, throwing out ideas, melodies, lyrics.

Aeon's fingers flew over the keys, Jay's rhythms grew tighter, and I poured everything I had into my guitar.We weren't just preparing for a song—we were preparing to make a statement. That our sound, our music, was still relevant. That we could stand toe-to-toe with the best of Angga's lineup and show them what Itchyworms Reborn was truly made of.By the time the weekend came around, I felt like we had a knife's edge to our sound—sharp, clear, and ready to cut through anything Angga threw our way.

Standing outside her studio, I looked over at Aeon and Jay. "Ready?"Jay cracked his knuckles. "Born ready."Aeon smiled, but there was a glint of steel in her eyes. "Let's show them what we've got."I nodded, pushing open the door and stepping inside. No more doubts. No more second-guessing.It was time to see if we could truly live up to the name of Itchyworms.

Chapter 11

The stadium loomed ahead, a giant structure pulsing with energy as we approached. I felt the anticipation build in my chest, mingling with nerves and excitement. This was it—our shot. As we made our way inside, I spotted Angga leaning against a wall, her presence magnetic, radiating an unsettling confidence. Beside her stood Laya, her beauty striking yet haunting, like a figure caught between allure and despair.

Her skin glowed under the harsh lights, and her figure seemed sculpted by an artist with a twisted vision. Next to her was her boyfriend, a chiseled figure reminiscent of a marble statue—perfect yet devoid of life, his expression unreadable. "Welcome, Itchyworms," Angga said, her voice smooth and commanding. "I'm glad you could make it. Are you ready for a little competition?" Laya's eyes flickered toward us, a sly smile creeping across her lips. "I hope you're prepared to lose," she said, her tone dripping with challenge.

Jay, ever the bold one, stepped forward, fists clenched at his sides. "We don't plan on going down easy. Just remember, it's not just a game. It's our music." The boyfriend shot Jay a sideways glance, his demeanor icy. "Hope your music can back up your bravado. It'd be a shame to see someone crash and burn." I could see the tension building, the air thickening as we stood on the brink of confrontation. Jay's eyes narrowed, but I sensed he chose not to engage. The stakes were higher than petty insults now, and we had to remain focused. Angga laid out the rules: one round, one hour, and the theme for our original song—love for someone who already has someone else.

The weight of her words settled heavily in the air, like an unspoken challenge. She leaned forward, her eyes glimmering with an intensity that demanded attention. "You see," Angga began, her voice dropping to a more intimate tone, "I once loved a man who was already committed to someone else. I thought I could hide my feelings, bury them deep beneath layers of indifference, but the heart doesn't lie. I watched them together, sharing laughter and moments that I yearned to be a part of. It was a beautiful yet agonizing experience—loving someone from afar, knowing they would never be mine." The room fell silent, our minds swirling with her story. Angga continued, her voice tinged with nostalgia, "I remember the songs that echoed my pain—how every melody felt like a reminder of what I couldn't have.

That's the essence I want you to capture in your piece: the bittersweet ache of unrequited love, the longing that lingers even when you know it's hopeless." As she spoke, the story seeped into my thoughts, mingling with the melody of "Akin Ka Nalang" that flickered in the back of my mind. Suddenly, the weight of her challenge felt even heavier. I had to create something that resonated with her experience, something that conveyed the emotional depth of love tinged with heartbreak. As we took our places, my mind raced with possibilities. I couldn't help but think of Angga's story—the pain of unrequited love, the longing for someone who belonged to another.

It resonated deeply, sparking memories I had tried to bury.I noticed Aeon standing nearby, her expression fixed as she listened intently to Angga. A flicker of emotion crossed her face—was it longing, or perhaps a hint of sadness? She seemed to relate to Angga's words on a profound level, and it tugged at my heart. The intensity of her gaze hinted at a deeper struggle, one that mirrored the unspoken sentiments I had sensed in her during my coma.I remembered the hushed confession that had slipped from her lips during a moment of vulnerability—how she had poured out her frustration over her feelings for someone who seemed just out of reach.

It was a bittersweet revelation, one that resonated through the fog of my memory. The weight of her words had lingered in the air, echoing with the same pain that Angga was now recounting.As I stood there, watching Aeon's expression flicker with emotions, memories of our past flooded my mind. I recalled those days when we were in the band together, the three of us—Jack, Aeon, and Jay—creating music that echoed our hopes and dreams.————One late night after practice, the air was thick with unspoken words.

Aeon and I had slipped away to the rooftop, the city lights twinkling beneath us like stars scattered across the ground. We sat side by side, our guitars resting in our laps, the cool breeze brushing against our skin. "Jack," she had said, her voice barely above a whisper, "can I ask you something?" I looked over, sensing the weight behind her words. "Of course, what's on your mind?" She took a deep breath, her gaze fixed on the horizon. "Do you ever think about us? About what we could be?" The question hung in the air, a delicate balance between hope and fear. My heart raced, but uncertainty clawed at my throat. "Aeon, I—" "I mean, I really like you, Jack," she interrupted, her eyes searching mine. "I think we could have something special if we tried." I felt a rush of warmth at her confession, but it was quickly followed by a pang of dread.

"Aeon, I care about you, I really do, but…" I hesitated, struggling to find the right words. "What about Jay? He's our friend. I don't want to mess that up." Her expression shifted, disappointment flashing across her features. "So, you don't want to explore this? We could make it work, I know we could." I shook my head, guilt twisting in my gut. "It's not that simple. I don't want to risk our friendship over something that might not last." For a moment, silence enveloped us, the weight of our unspoken feelings hanging heavily in the air. We had shared laughter, dreams, and a deep bond, but crossing that line felt too dangerous. I could see the longing in her eyes, but I was too afraid to embrace it. "I get it," she said finally, her voice trembling slightly. "I just thought… maybe we could try."—--As the words slipped away, I could see the flicker of hurt in her gaze.

I felt like I was breaking something precious, but I convinced myself it was for the best.Now, as I watched Aeon's reaction, the echoes of that night resonated in my heart. The memory of her earnest confession lingered, a reminder of a love we never fully explored. Despite our choice to remain friends, I could see now that the desire for something more still simmered beneath the surface, a longing that had never truly faded.I wanted to reach out and comfort her, to assure her that she wasn't alone in this over-whelming tide of emotions. But at that moment, I was drowning in my own turmoil—the pressure of the competition, the desperate need to recall the lyrics, and the haunting echoes of Angga's story swirled in my mind like a tempest.

The memory of Aeon's confession the night I got hit by a truck and got comatosed also pressed against my heart. Though I only vaguely remember the words she said, I wished I could tell her that I understood her pain, that I too had felt the ache of long-ing—though my heart belonged to another. I loved Dina fiercely, and yet I could sense the weight of unrequited love in Aeon's expression, the heavy burden she carried for someone who felt forever out of reach. But the words caught in my throat, stifled by my own uncertainty. How could I comfort her when my heart was so intricately tied to my wife, a love that was both a refuge and a source of guilt?I turned to Aeon and Jay, trying to mask the whirlwind of thoughts swirling in my head.

"Hey, what do you think about me performing solo this time?" I asked, keeping my voice steady. "With the time crunch, it might be better if I just go for it alone. You know, give it my all without any distractions."They exchanged glances, uncertainty flickering across their faces. "You sure, Jack?" Jay replied, his brow furrowing in concern."Yeah, but we don't have the luxury of time today. I'll be able to focus better and really pour everything into the performance," I insisted, even though my heart raced with the pressure of recalling the lyrics and melody.Aeon looked hesitant but nodded. "If you think that's best, we trust you, Jack. Just... make it count, okay?"I forced a smile, grateful for their faith in me.

"I will. Just... give me a moment." I stepped back, closing my eyes for a brief second to clear my mind, but the lyrics danced just out of reach. I had to dig deep, find that connection to Angga's story, and turn it into something that resonated with all of us.Laya was up first. As she stepped forward, her presence captivated the room. The moment she opened her mouth, a beautiful melody flowed out, enchanting everyone in attendance. But as her lyrics unfolded, I felt a growing dissonance. The words, while lovely, didn't connect to the theme. Angga's expression shifted from admiration to confusion, her brow furrowing as she tried to find a thread of relatability in Laya's performance."

"Come on, Jack," I thought, forcing myself to focus. I had to find a way to translate Angga's experience into music."Hey, you've got this," Jay said, his voice low but steady, breaking through my thoughts."Just remember why you're here. Make it count."I glanced at him, grateful for the support but feeling the weight of my own expectations. "Thanks, man. I'll do my best," I replied, trying to sound more confident than I felt. Deep down, I knew I had to channel all my emotions into this performance — not just for Angga, but for Dina, Aeon and for the memories that lingered in the back of my mind.As Laya finished, I felt the pressure of time closing in on me.

I closed my eyes, desperately searching my mind for the perfect melody.Akin Ka Nalang. It was there, dancing just beyond my grasp, begging to be recalled. The seconds ticked away as I played the notes in my head, piecing together the fragments of lyrics, hoping I could shape it into something meaningful.Aeon and Jay were watching me intently, their faith in me unwavering. I felt their support like a lifeline, pushing me to keep going.Finally, it was my turn. I took a deep breath, my heart pounding in rhythm with my guitar. As I strummed the first chords of Akin Ka Nalang, I altered the tempo, shifting it into a slow, lovely melody.

Each note reverberated with the emotions I felt—love, longing, and the bittersweet ache of knowing someone belongs to another.As I poured my heart into the performance, the melody wove through the air, carrying the weight of Angga's story alongside my own. I remembered every moment with Dina, the laughter we shared, and the painful memories of our past. I thought of Aeon too, of the complicated feelings that lingered between us, the unspoken words that could never be said.As the last notes faded into the silence, I caught a glimpse of Angga. Her expression shifted, her eyes glistening as the song connected with her. I could see memories surfacing in her gaze, perhaps reminding her of her own unfulfilled desires.

I poured every ounce of emotion into my performance, weaving a tapestry of yearning that I hoped would resonate with everyone.When I finished, I bowed, feeling a rush of relief. The applause that followed was drowned out by my thoughts. But before I could retreat backstage, Laya approached me, her smile wide and flirtatious. "Wow, Jack, that was incredible!" she exclaimed, her tone flirty as she tilted her head slightly, her eyes sparkling with mischief."I didn't realize you had such talent. That song was... for me, right?"I simply smiled, unsure how to respond.

Did she really think the song was meant for her? I shook my head slightly, a mix of amusement and confusion swirling inside me.With that, I turned away, the tension in my chest tightening as I spotted Dina in the audience. I made my way towards her, needing the comfort of her presence. The confusion and guilt swirled in my mind like a storm, and I needed to ground myself before I lost my way entirely.As I approached, I caught Aeon's gaze, and a flicker of something unreadable passed between us.

I felt the weight of her feelings, but I brushed it aside. Dina smiled up at me, and in that moment, everything else faded away. Her presence reminded me of the love that anchored me."Jack, you were amazing!" she exclaimed, her eyes shining with pride."Th anks, love," I replied, wrapping my arms around her. Her warmth enveloped me, reminding me of the life we shared together. "I couldn't have done it without your support."Angga stepped onto the stage, her voice commanding the crowd's attention.

"The winner, Itchyworms! You moved me with your song, and I believe you all have the potential to explore your musical direction freely!"A mix of relief and joy washed over me, but Laya was not done. She approached once more, her gaze playful. "Congrats! But just so you know, I might just break up with my boyfriend. I could see us together, you know?"I chuckled softly, feeling a little flustered. "That's nice, but I'm married," I said, trying to keep it light."Doesn't matter to me," she replied, her tone teasing yet insistent.I felt a rush of warmth at her compliment, but guilt twisted in my gut as I thought of Dina.I shook my head, a smile on my face as I stepped back toward my bandmates, my heart still racing from the performance. The music battle had come to a close, but something told me this was just the beginning of a much larger journey ahead.

Chapter 12

The whirlwind of fame hit Itchyworms like a tidal wave. One moment, we were just a group of friends making music in a dimly lit garage, and the next, we were playing gigs back-to-back, our names lighting up marquees across the city. Each night was filled with the electric energy of the crowd, the spotlight bathing us in its warm glow, but underneath the excitement lurked a tangle of emotions that I struggled to unravel.

I would finish a show, the echoes of applause still ringing in my ears, and my mind would immediately drift to Dina. It felt wrong to revel in success while she sat at home, her world shrinking to the four walls of our living room, the vibrant woman I fell in love with now confined to a wheelchair. She had been my rock, my muse. How could I enjoy the high of the crowd without sharing it with her?

I found myself staring at my phone more than ever, half-hoping for a text or call from her, yet fully aware that I was being a terrible husband. My hands trembled as I thought about her, memories flooding in—her laughter, her smiles, the way she used to tease me about my terrible dance moves. I tried to call her whenever I could, but every conversation ended with me feeling more like a stranger in my own home.

Every time I walked onto a stage, a piece of me felt like it was missing.

The latest gig was in a packed arena, the buzz of anticipation humming in the air. As I stood backstage, my heart raced. Aeon was beside me, her excitement palpable as she adjusted her hair in the mirror. Jay was tuning his drums, the familiar sound echoing like a heartbeat in the background.

"Are you ready?" Aeon asked, her voice laced with an infectious enthusiasm.

I offered a smile, but the weight of my thoughts lingered. "Yeah, I guess so."

"Guess? C'mon, Jack! We're gonna rock this!" she said, giving my shoulder a playful shove.

"Right," I replied, trying to muster the same excitement she exuded.

As we stepped onto the stage, the lights blared down, blinding for a moment before the crowd came into view. Thousands of faces, all screaming for us. It was intoxicating, yet, as I strummed the first chords of our opening song, a familiar ache pulled at my chest. I caught a glimpse of Aeon beside me, her energy radiating like a beacon. The way she moved, the way she sang—it reminded me of the late-night jam sessions we used to have, where it was just us and the music.

But with every note I played, my heart remained anchored to Dina, to the life I had left behind in pursuit of this fleeting fame.

After the show, the adrenaline still coursing through me, I joined Aeon and Jay in the green room, the air thick with the smell of sweat and triumph. Fans were clamoring for pictures and autographs, and the buzz of our victory over the competition still hung in the air.

"Did you see their faces?" Jay laughed, wiping his brow with a towel. "They loved us!"

"Yeah, it was great," I said, though my smile felt strained.

Aeon nudged me. "What's up with you? You should be celebrating!"

"I am, it's just... I can't stop thinking about Dina."

Her expression softened, but I noticed a flicker of something in her eyes—was it annoyance? "You need to let her go for a bit, Jack. She wouldn't want you to be miserable when you have all of this," she gestured around at the vibrant chaos of the room.

I shook my head, feeling the weight of her words. "I can't just forget about her. She's my wife."

"Just... think about it," she replied, her voice softer. "You deserve happiness too."

Days turned into weeks, and our schedule only got busier. With every gig, I felt a growing distance between Dina and me. I knew she was struggling. I could see the loneliness etched on her face through the screen of our calls, even if she tried to smile for me. Each time I hung up, the guilt gnawed at me like a persistent itch I couldn't scratch.

One evening, as we prepared for yet another live TV appearance, I caught myself staring at the mirror, trying to convince myself that everything was okay. Aeon was running through her lines beside me, but my thoughts were elsewhere—far away from the bright lights and the audience, back to the soft embrace of our home.

"Hey, Jack, you okay?" Aeon asked, breaking my reverie.

"Yeah, just... thinking."

"About Dina?"

I nodded, unable to mask my frustration. "I don't know how to balance all of this. I feel like I'm failing her."

Aeon stepped closer, her eyes searching mine. "You're not failing her. You're just trying to figure it out. It's a lot, but you can't be everything for everyone. You have to take care of yourself too."

I wanted to argue, to defend my position, but deep down, I knew she was right. I just wished I didn't feel so lost.

The TV studio was buzzing with energy. Cameras flashed, and the host, a charismatic figure with a megawatt smile, greeted us with enthusiasm.

"Welcome, Itchyworms!" she exclaimed, her voice cutting through the noise. "You've become the talk of the town! Your recent win has everyone buzzing. Tell us, how does it feel to be on top?"

Jay and Aeon shared a laugh, but I felt an unfamiliar tension coil in my stomach. "It feels great," I managed to say, trying to match their enthusiasm.

The host turned to Aeon, her eyes sparkling. "You two have such great chemistry on stage. Is there something more between you and Jack?"

Before I could respond, Aeon smiled brightly and said, "Yes! We're a thing!"

Gasps filled the studio as the audience erupted into applause and chatter. My heart sank.

"Wait, what?" I stammered, caught off guard.

The host leaned in, eyes wide with intrigue. "Is that true? Are you two officially together?"

I opened my mouth to deny it, to clarify the misunderstanding, but the words stuck in my throat. I glanced at Aeon, who was still beaming, clearly enjoying the attention. The buzz around us only grew louder.

The host leaned closer. "What do you say, Jack? Are you and Aeon an item?"

"No!" I finally burst out, my voice rising above the noise. "I mean, not like that—"

Aeon placed a hand on my arm, but the warmth didn't reach my heart. "It's okay, Jack. I just wanted to have some fun with it," she said, her voice low.

The moment hung heavy in the air, filled with anticipation and confusion. I was furious. How could she say that? How could she put me in this position, especially when I was already wrestling with my feelings for her?

After the segment wrapped, I stormed off set, the echoes of the audience still buzzing in my ears. My heart raced with a mix of anger and confusion. How could Aeon say something like that? Once I got back in the green room, I saw Aeon and Jay already there.

I whirled to face Aeon. "What were you thinking?"

"What were you thinking?"

Jay suddenly stood up, sensing the tension in the air. "I know where this is going. I'm gonna go out and give you guys the room," he said hastily, slipping out before I could stop him.

"I was just having fun, Jack! It's not like you're the only one who feels something here!" she snapped back, her voice sharp.

"Fun? This is my life we're talking about! What about Dina?"

Her expression shifted, and for a moment, I saw vulnerability in her eyes. "Dina isn't here, is she? You need to live a little. I'm not saying you should forget about her, but you're not doing yourself any favors by shutting me out."

I took a step back, her words hitting harder than I anticipated. "I'm not shutting you out. I love Dina, and I'm trying to be there for her, even if it's not in person."

"And what if you want more than just to be her husband? What if you want someone who's actually here, who can support you through this? Just because she's not around doesn't mean you should ignore what you feel!"

I was furious. "You think I want this? To feel torn between my wife and someone I care about?"

"I think you need to be honest with yourself, Jack," she shot back, her voice rising. "You can't keep pretending this isn't happening. You and I have something special, and I can't just ignore it!"

I stood there, my heart racing, feeling completely out of control. "No, Aeon! I can't be with you. Not like this."

Her face fell, and for a brief moment, I saw a flash of disappointment. "Why not?" she challenged, crossing her arms. "Why can't you just let yourself be happy for once?"

I shook my head, my breath quickening. "I can't just be your man while Dina isn't around. That's not fair to her. It's not fair to any of us."

I turned and left the room, my mind a whirlwind of anger, confusion, and guilt. I needed to talk to Dina. I needed to hear her voice, even if it was over the phone.

I stepped outside into the cool night air, my heart racing as I dialed Dina's number. The familiar ring echoed in my ears, each sound sending a fresh wave of guilt crashing over me.

"Hello?" Her voice came through, warm and inviting yet laced with an undercurrent of sadness.

"Dina, hey. It's me," I said, trying to keep my tone light.

"Hey, Jack. How was the show?"

"It was great, but—" I hesitated, my thoughts swirling. I had so much to say, but where to begin?

"But what?" she pressed, her voice quiet.

"I need to talk to you about something. About Aeon."

I could hear her intake of breath, a long pause stretching between us. "Oh."

"I didn't want you to hear it on TV. It was just—she was caught up in the moment, and I didn't mean to let it happen. I love you, Dina. You know that, right?"

Silence followed. My heart pounded as I waited for her response, each second stretching into eternity.

"Yeah, I know," she said finally, her voice barely above a whisper.

"I would never choose anyone over you. It's just—things are complicated here. I'm trying to balance everything, and I feel like I'm failing you," I admitted, my voice cracking.

"Jack, I see what's happening. You're trying to keep us afloat while living this new life. I can't ask you to stop living your dreams just because I can't be there," she said, and the resignation in her tone broke my heart.

"That's not what I want," I said urgently. "I want you here with me, I want to share all of this with you, but I feel like I'm being pulled in two directions."

"I'm proud of you, you know," she said softly, the warmth of her words washing over me. "You've worked so hard, and I don't want to hold you back. Just... be honest with me, okay?"

"I will," I promised, but the weight of our reality loomed over us, thick and heavy.

"Just remember, Jack, I'm always in your corner. No matter what happens," she said, her voice steady despite the distance between us.

As I hung up, the feeling of helplessness clawed at me. I wanted to make everything right, to balance the scales of my life, but I had no idea how.

Returning to the venue, I found Aeon leaning against the wall, her expression unreadable.

"Jack," she said quietly, pushing off the wall as I approached.

"I talked to Dina," I replied, my voice hoarse. "She's understand-ing, but I feel like I'm losing her."

Aeon sighed, crossing her arms. "I'm sorry for what I said. I didn't mean to push you. I just... I care about you."

"I know you do, but I can't do this right now. Not when she's still in my life," I said firmly.

"Okay," she replied, leaning closer. A chill ran down my spine—not from the cold air, but from the intensity of her gaze. "But just know that I'm here if you need someone."

With that, she turned and walked away, leaving me feeling even more lost than before. I watched her disappear into the crowd, the distance between us growing with every step she took. Her parting words echoed in my mind, intertwining with an unsettling thought: what if Dina was no longer my wife?

The notion caught me off guard, twisting my gut. I pictured our life together—the shared dreams, the laughter, the little moments that stitched us into each other's lives. Losing her felt like a knife cutting through my being. But what if she were alive, yet we were no longer bound by marriage? The world around me blurred as I considered the implications.

What if Dina became a ghost in my life, a reminder of everything I once held dear but without her warmth? I could still see her smile and hear her laughter, but I'd be haunted by the fact that we were just two people sharing the same space, no longer committed to each other. The love we had would morph into something foreign, a specter of what once was.

This thought ignited a fear that coursed through me, as if I were staring into a void where our future should have been. I could picture myself sitting across from her at the dinner table, silence stretching between us, filled with unsaid words and unresolved feelings. How could I navigate a life where the woman I loved was still there, yet emotionally, she felt miles away?

And what would that mean for me? Could I explore these feelings for Aeon if Dina was no longer my wife in any meaningful way? The guilt crept in, wrapping around my heart like a constrictor, squeezing until it was hard to breathe. Would I be abandoning Dina in her time of need?

As I pondered this unsettling prospect, I realized such a reality would change everything. The choices I made, the path I walked—it all hinged on my connection with Dina. If that bond were severed, what would be left? Would I become just another man chasing something new while leaving the wreckage of my past behind? I couldn't shake the weight of this thought, a shadow looming over me, whispering that the deeper I delved into my feelings for Aeon, the further I would stray from the love that had once anchored me. A love that felt like a fading memory.

The following days blurred into a haze of performances and media appearances. Jack and I found ourselves in the spotlight more than ever, and while the fame was intoxicating, the reality of my relationship with Dina loomed like a shadow. I felt like I was living two lives, one on stage and one at home.

Despite the chaos, I couldn't shake the nagging feeling that something needed to change. My heart longed for the simplicity of the life I once knew, but the music called to me in ways I couldn't ignore.

One evening, after yet another successful gig, I found myself alone in the quiet of my hotel room, the weight of loneliness pressing down on me. The phone buzzed on the nightstand—Dina's name lighting up the screen, and I felt a flutter of hope mixed with anxiety.

"Hey, babe," I answered, forcing a steadiness into my voice that I didn't quite feel.

"Hey, Jack. How was the show?" she asked, her tone laced with something that felt like apprehension.

"It was incredible, but I miss you," I admitted, the longing swelling in my chest. The silence that followed felt heavy, as if the distance between us had grown impossibly vast.

"I miss you too," she replied, though the slight tremor in her voice made it clear that all was not well. "How did it go?"

"It was just Aeon and me, actually. Jay was a no-show," I said, trying to keep the mood light, but the weight of her silence pressed down on me.

"Just the two of you," she echoed, her tone shifting to something sharper. "I hope it wasn't too... intimate."

The accusation stung. "Not like that," I rushed to reassure her, though I could feel the tension in my own voice. "It went well, but it wasn't the same without Jay. I miss the whole vibe of the band."

"Well, you're doing amazing things," she said, her voice tinged with frustration. I could sense the jealousy creeping in, and it made my heart race. "Just keep chasing your dreams, I guess."

"I will," I promised, though the emptiness gnawed at me, a constant reminder of what I was missing back home. The room felt stifling, my thoughts a chaotic jumble of guilt and desire.

Suddenly, a loud bang echoed in the background, startling Dina. "What was that? Who's there?" she asked, her voice tight with worry.

"Probably just a cat," I brushed it off, trying to maintain a facade of calm.

"Promise me you'll be careful, Jack," she urged, her words wrapping around me like a fragile thread. "I love you so much—more than you'll ever know. Goodbye for now." Her voice carried a depth of emotion that hit me like a wave, and I felt tears prick at the corners of my eyes.

"Wait, I—" I started, but before I could finish, Aeon burst into the room, her playful energy flooding the space. "What's this? Missing me already?" she teased, her eyes sparkling with mischief.

Just as I turned to respond, she jumped into my line of sight, causing the phone to slip from my hand. "I lo—" I shouted, my voice trailing off as the phone hit the floor, the connection severed in an instant.

The sound of Aeon's flirty remark lingered in the air, a haunting echo that left me with a mix of guilt and confusion. My heart raced as I knelt to retrieve the phone, knowing I had just let the most important conversation slip through my fingers.

The weight of my choices hung heavily on me, pulling me in two directions — one toward the warmth and familiarity of Dina, and the other toward the intoxicating thrill of something new with Aeon. I felt trapped in a whirlwind of emotions, the realization that I was caught in a dangerous game of desire, one that could shatter everything I held dear.

Chapter 13

As the call ended, I felt the familiar tightness in my chest. "Just remember, Jack, I'm always in your corner. No matter what happens," I had said, trying to infuse my words with strength. But inside, I was unraveling. I gripped the armrests of my wheelchair tightly, the cold metal biting into my palms, anchoring me to the present. Jack's laughter echoed in my mind, but it felt distant, like a song fading into silence. I closed my eyes, trying to summon the warmth of our shared moments, but all I felt was the heavy weight of uncertainty pressing down on me.

The truth clawed at me: Jack was drifting, and the more I thought about it, the heavier my heart became. His laughter, his passion for music—was it for me anymore, or was it meant for her? Aeon. I could almost feel her shadow looming between us, whispering doubts into my ear, fueling my insecurities. Did Jack confide in her? Did he share the dreams we had built together, or were those dreams slipping away, one note at a time?

I closed my eyes, trying to shake off the spiraling thoughts. But then, like a door flung open, memories came rushing back—memories of a time when I was whole, before the world became a cruel reminder of what I had lost.

The venue was alive with energy that night, and I sat in the cramped dressing room, excitement buzzing in the air. Jack was on stage with Aeon and Jay, their music pulsing through the walls, electrifying the crowd. I could hear the cheers outside, but inside, I felt a strange mix of anticipation and anxiety.

"Dina, are you ready?" Jack had asked just moments before, his smile bright, illuminating the dim room.

"I can't wait to see you perform!" I replied, my heart swelling with pride.

But then, disaster struck. A deafening crash echoed through the building, and the lights flickered ominously. I felt the ground shake beneath me, and my heart raced as I realized something was horribly wrong. Smoke filled the air, thick and choking. My instincts screamed at me to run, but the dressing room door wouldn't budge.

"Help! Someone, please!" I cried, panic clawing at my throat. The flames surged closer, devouring everything in their path. I tried to push the door open again, but the heat pressed against me, making it impossible to escape. My eyes darted around the small space, desperately searching for a way out. But all I found was darkness closing in.

Then, it happened—a massive burning pillar crashed down, trapping me beneath it. Pain exploded in my waist, and I gasped, a scream caught in my throat. I could barely move; despair washed over me like a tidal wave. As I lay there, helpless and terrified, I caught a glimpse of Jack through the haze. His face, filled with determination, as he fought to reach me.

"Dina!" he shouted, and in that moment, I knew he would save me. But the damage was done.

I jolted back to the present, my heart racing. The memories flooded my mind, each one a reminder of the day everything changed. That fire had taken my ability to walk and, in many ways, my place in Jack's life. I had become the rock he leaned on, but now it felt like I was being overshadowed by a boulder—his burgeoning career, his connection with Aeon.

Days passed in a blur of self-doubt and pain. I wanted to be part of Jack's success, to share in the joy of his achievements, but I felt the distance between us grow wider with each passing moment. It was as if I were standing on one side of an endless chasm, watching him on the other, reaching for dreams that no longer included me.

Then, as if summoned by my spiraling thoughts, my phone rang. It was Jack again.

"Hey, babe," He answered, forcing a steadiness into his voice that I didn't quite feel.

"Hey, Jack. How was the show?" I asked, my tone laced with apprehension.

"It was incredible, but I miss you," he admitted, the longing swelling in his chest. The silence that followed felt heavy, as if the distance between us had grown impossibly vast.

"I miss you too," I replied, though the slight tremor in my voice made it clear that all was not well.

"How did it go?"

"It was just Aeon and me, actually. Jay was a no-show,"

Hearing him say it was just the two of them sent a stab of insecurity through me. My mind raced with images of them alone together, laughter echoing in a way that felt intimate and foreign. The tension in his voice hinted at something unsaid, something that gnawed at my insides. I wanted to trust him, but a part of me couldn't shake the feeling that I was losing him to her.

"Just the two of you," I echoed, my heart racing. "I hope it wasn't too... intimate."

The words slipped out sharper than I intended, a reflection of my rising insecurities. A chill crept up my spine, and I could feel my pulse quickening with each passing moment. Jack's laughter, the warmth of their shared moments, haunted me like a ghost. Was it wrong to feel this way? I tried to suppress the swell of jealousy, but it clawed at me, raw and unyielding. The very thought of him and Aeon sharing a bond I felt excluded from twisted like a knife in my gut.

The accusation stung.

"Not like that," he rushed to reassure me, but I could hear the uncertainty in his voice. "It went well, but it wasn't the same without Jay. I miss the whole vibe of the band."

"Well, you're doing amazing things," I said, frustration lacing my words. The jealousy that clawed at me made my heart race. "Just keep chasing your dreams, I guess."

"I will," he promised, though I could hear the emptiness in his voice, a constant reminder of what we were losing.

As I spoke, I felt a sinking sensation deep within me. Every word hung heavy in the air, like a chain dragging us both down. The dream Jack was pursuing felt like it was pulling him further away from me, away from our shared life and the love we once celebrated together.

I wanted to be his support, his rock, but now I worried I was just a weight holding him back. The thought twisted my insides, the feeling of inadequacy gnawing at me. He was thriving, while I felt stagnant and trapped in this life I didn't choose. What if chasing those dreams meant losing him entirely?

My heart ached at the possibility, my mind racing with doubts and fears, drowning in an overwhelming tide of insecurity.

Suddenly, a loud bang echoed in the background, startling me.

"What was that? Who's there?" I asked, my voice tight with worry.

"Probably just a cat," he brushed it off, trying to maintain a facade of calm, but it felt like a weak excuse. I could sense that he didn't really care about the noise; it was just another distraction from the tension between us.

My heart sank as I realized that the sound—whatever it was—had become another insignificant detail in his busy life, overshadowed by the excitement of his career. Did he even notice how the chaos around us mirrored the turmoil in our relationship?

It stung to think that something so trivial could slip by unnoticed, just like my fears and insecurities.

"Promise me you'll be careful, Jack," I urged, fear creeping into my chest. "I love you so much—more than you'll ever know. Goodbye for now."

My words carried a depth of emotion that hit me like a wave, and I felt tears prick at the corners of my eyes. As I ended the call, the weight of doubt settled back into my bones. Jack's laughter echoed in my mind, but it felt distant, like a song fading into silence.

I couldn't shake the feeling that I was losing him to Aeon's allure.

Then, out of nowhere, the sound of a loud bang resonated outside, shattering the quiet. Panic surged within me. I pushed myself to see, breath hitching in my throat as I saw my store in the garage engulfed in flames.

"No, no, no!" I gasped, scrambling for my phone, trying to call for help, but my hands trembled. The fire roared, an inferno hungry for everything in its path. I needed to escape, but the entrances were already consumed. My heart raced with a primal fear, and I tried to reach emergency services.

In my panic, I hit the last known caller feature, praying it was Jack.

"Please, please," I whispered, but the call wouldn't go through. Fear wrapped around me like a vice, and I was paralyzed—again. The flames surged closer, licking at the walls of my prison, and I was trapped in a burning cage, unable to save myself or reach him.

The heat was suffocating, a familiar and horrific reminder of that night when everything changed. I could almost hear the panicked screams, the crackling fire, and the smell of smoke that had choked me back then. In my mind, I was back in that dressing room, the world spinning out of control as I struggled to escape.

A pillar had fallen, crushing me beneath its weight, pinning me to the ground. I could feel the searing heat seeping through my skin, igniting a pain that transcended the physical. The memory flooded my senses, engulfing me in a tidal wave of despair and helplessness. I fought to breathe, to call out for help, but my voice was lost amid the chaos.

As the fire consumed the room, I thought of Jack, of our love—the laughter we shared, the whispered dreams we had woven together like a tapestry of hope.

Each memory flashed before my eyes like a flickering flame, illuminating the darkness that threatened to swallow me whole. Would he remember me as the woman who stood steadfast in his corner, cheering him on through every triumph? Or would I become another lost memory, a flicker extinguished by the flames of jealousy and ambition, relegated to the shadows of his past?

In those final moments, the heat intensified, and I could feel the flames dancing around me, mocking my helplessness. My heart raced with an all-consuming fear, but beneath it lay a fragile hope: Jack would come for me, just as he had before. I could almost picture him bursting through the door, his eyes wide with concern, ready to save me from this nightmare once again.

He would pull me into his arms, shield me from the flames, and together we would escape into the light of a new dawn. But the truth was bitter. As the smoke thickened and the fire roared, I realized that he wasn't coming for me. Instead, he was out there, with Aeon, perhaps laughing and flirting in a way that felt more carnal than I could bear to imagine.

The thought twisted like a knife in my heart, intensifying the flames of my jealousy. Was I just a fading memory to him, a woman lost to the shadows of his burgeoning success? I was alone, trapped in this burning cage of memories and regrets, with every heartbeat echoing the unrelenting truth: Jack had chosen a different path.

I could almost hear the laughter of their shared moments drifting through the crackling fire, a haunting reminder of what I could never reclaim. The love we had built together felt like a distant echo now, replaced by the inferno that consumed me, both literally and metaphorically.

As the heat pressed against my skin and the smoke clawed at my throat, I wondered if he would ever realize the weight of my sacrifice. Would he remember the woman who had stood by him, who believed in him when he felt lost? Or would I simply be another casualty in the blaze of his ambitions, a flicker snuffed out by the flames of jealousy and abandonment?

But even in those suffocating moments, as despair threatened to consume me, a part of me clung to the truth: no matter what Jack chose—whether it was fame, Aeon, or something entirely different—I would still accept him.

I would always be there, the rock in his life amidst the shifting sands and pebbles of his ambitions. My love for him was steadfast and unyielding, a beacon in the dark, reminding me that true love endures even as the flames threatened to consume me.

Whatever path he chose, I would always be there, waiting in the shadows. Yet, as the heat intensified and the smoke thickened, I realized this time, I might not escape. I could become a whisper in his memories, a flickering image against the brilliance of his dreams.

Still, even in the face of my demise, my heart swelled with love for him. No matter the distance between us, he would carry a piece of me. I would remain his rock, forever cheering him on, even if it meant watching him shine without me.

"I love you, Jack. Goodbye." The words escaped my lips, a whispered prayer to the universe as the flames roared around me.

Chapter 14

The sound of Aeon's flirty remark lingered in the air, a haunting echo that left me with a mix of guilt and confusion. My heart raced as I knelt to retrieve the phone, knowing I had just let the most important conversation slip through my fingers. The broken screen reflected my fractured emotions, shards of feelings scattered within me.

As I picked up the pieces of my phone, I couldn't shake the weight of my choices. It pulled me in two directions—one toward the warmth and familiarity of Dina, the love that had anchored my life for so long, and the other toward the intoxicating thrill of something new with Aeon, a dangerous distraction I wasn't sure I could afford. I felt trapped in a whirlwind of emotions, caught in a dangerous game of desire, one that could shatter everything I held dear.

I glared at the shattered device in my hand, frustration boiling over. "What the hell, Aeon?" I spat, the anger surging through me.

Aeon tilted her head, an innocent look on her face that was anything but. "Oh, come on, Jack. Don't be such a downer. "I'll repay you with my body," she said, her voice low as she leaned closer, our faces inches apart, almost touching lips. Aeon puts her hands on my shoulder, while her left arm slowly trails down to my navel, sending a jolt of electricity through me. Just as her fingers neared the waistband of my pants, she jumped back, a playful grin lighting up her face. "Just kidding!" she winked, the sudden shift from tension to playfulness disarmed me. "I'll buy you a new phone instead."

I blinked at her, the tension between us thick enough to cut with a knife. My heart raced not just from her words, but from the conflicting feelings that swirled within me. Was this how I was supposed to feel? Flattered? Angry? All I could manage was a terse, "Just leave me alone, Aeon."

As I turned away from her, the remnants of my phone still clutched in my hand, I felt a storm brewing within. I needed to escape, to drown out the noise of my conflicting emotions. I sank into sleep, my mind a chaotic tangle of thoughts.

As I drifted into sleep, I found myself back in Mayari's domain. This time, it felt different—heavy, almost suffocating. The vibrant colors that had once danced around me were replaced by muted, shadowy hues. The air was thick, pressing down on me like a weight I couldn't shake off, every breath a struggle against the dense energy that surrounded me.

I glanced around, noting how the once-enchanting landscape now felt oppressive, as if the very essence of the place had absorbed the sorrow I carried in my heart. Gone were the lively bursts of color that had filled my previous visits; instead, the world felt draped in a shroud of melancholy, each corner echoing the weight of despair.

This wasn't the Mayari I remembered. Where once I had marveled at the beauty and magic of her realm, now I felt an uncomfortable sense of loss, as though the domain itself mourned alongside me.

Mayari stood before me, her ethereal presence still striking, but her usual radiant glow was dimmed. Her eyes, once vibrant with the light of the moon, now held a sadness that mirrored my own. There was a heaviness in her expression, as if she understood the weight of my heartache and bore some of it herself. Her normally playful demeanor was replaced by a quiet sorrow that wrapped around her like a veil.

"Is this reality to your liking, Jack?" she asked, her voice smooth as silk, yet laced with an undercurrent of melancholy.

I hesitated, the question hanging in the air between us like the dense fog surrounding the domain. "I like it here," I finally admitted, though my voice sounded hollow even to my ears. "There are ups and downs to this reality, but I am someone here. I'm famous."

Mayari's gaze pierced through me, searching for the truth behind my words. "Is fame what really matters to you?" she asked, tilting her head slightly, her long, dark hair cascading like a waterfall around her shoulders. "What about the rocks that serve as your foundation?"

I shrugged, trying to dismiss the weight of her question. "I can just pick up the rocks that fall, right?"

"But what if the rock falls too far out of reach?" she pressed, her voice soft yet firm.

Her words struck a chord deep within me, and I found myself at a loss for a response. I had always believed I could handle any challenge, pick up the pieces of my life as they scattered. But the truth was, the thought of losing Dina felt like a rock tumbling into an abyss I couldn't reach.

Just then, a jolt pulled me from that world, and I awoke abruptly. The room was dark, the shadows looming larger than life. It took me a moment to gather my bearings, to remember the fragments of my dream.

"Jack!" Aeon's voice broke through the silence, She was standing in the doorway, her face pale and drawn, sadness etched into her features.

"What is it?" I asked, irritation lacing my tone. My heart sank, sensing that something was wrong.

"The news..." Her voice cracked, and she stepped closer, as if to shield herself from the weight of the words she was about to say. "Dina... she was caught in a fire."

The world tilted beneath me, a sickening sensation washing over me as her words sunk in. "What?" My voice barely rose above a whisper. "What are you talking about?"

Aeon's eyes glistened with unshed tears. "She didn't make it, Jack. She died."

Time froze. I felt as if the ground had been ripped from beneath my feet, leaving me suspended in a void of disbelief. The walls closed in around me, suffocating. I couldn't process it. I couldn't breathe.

"No. No. You're lying!" I shot back, desperation clawing at my chest. "She can't be gone. We were just talking on the phone, She can't."

But as I searched Aeon's eyes, I saw the truth reflected back at me. The anguish, the sorrow — she wasn't lying. My mind raced back to all those moments I had taken for granted: Dina's laughter, her warmth, the way she made the world feel a little less heavy.

"I need to see her," I choked out, the realization crashing over me like a tidal wave. The love I had for Dina surged through me, strong and unyielding. She was my rock, the only one who truly mattered in this chaotic world. The thought of losing her was like being swept away in a storm, tossed and turned until I could no longer find my footing.

Aeon stepped closer, her expression softening. "I'm so sorry, Jack." Her hand reached out, but I recoiled, anger and pain battling within me. I couldn't take comfort from her. Not now.

In that moment, it became clear: without Dina, everything else was just shifting sands, ready to be swept away. Aeon, my fame, everything—none of it mattered. I was left with an emptiness so profound it felt like a chasm had opened in my chest.

"I can't believe this is happening," I muttered, feeling a heaviness settle over me like a dark cloud. "She's gone."

The words felt foreign on my tongue, and yet they hung in the air, a cruel reminder of my reality. I sank onto the edge of the bed, the weight of despair pressing down on me.

The darkness enveloped me, pulling me into its embrace. I wanted to scream, to lash out at the unfairness of it all, but instead, I sat there, lost in my grief. All those moments with Dina, all the dreams we had shared—they were gone, extinguished like a candle snuffed out in an instant.

The reality of my situation crashed down on me like a tidal wave, threatening to drag me under. I could almost hear Dina's laughter echoing in my mind, a sweet melody that felt so distant now. I thought about her warmth, her smile that could light up even the darkest days. Each memory felt like a knife twisting in my heart, reminding me of the vibrant life that had been extinguished too soon.

I remembered the moments we shared—the quiet evenings, the laughter over coffee, the plans we had for our future. All of it seemed like a cruel joke now. My heart ached with a longing I couldn't quite articulate, a yearning for the life we had built together. She was my rock, my anchor in a world that often felt chaotic and uncertain. Without her, I felt like a ship adrift at sea, lost in a storm without a destination.

I was pulled back to a moment from our honeymoon. The sun had just dipped below the horizon, casting a warm glow in our cozy hotel room. We lay entwined in each other's arms, the soft sheets cradling us in a peaceful embrace.

"Jack," Dina whispered, her voice barely above a murmur. "What do you think makes a relationship strong?"

I turned to her, surprised by the question. "I think it's trust and communication. And love, of course," I replied, watching her eyes sparkle in the dim light. "But love isn't just a feeling; it's a choice we make every day."

Dina smiled, a soft blush creeping across her cheeks. "So, you're saying we have to keep choosing each other?"

"Exactly," I said, brushing a strand of hair from her face. "Every day, no matter what happens, we choose to love each other. It's what makes us stronger. Till Death Do Us Part."

As I recalled that moment, the weight of grief pressed down on me, a reminder of the choices I had made and the life I had wanted to build with her. Now, those dreams lay shattered, the fragments piercing my heart like shards of glass, each memory a painful reminder of what I had lost. It was as if the universe had conspired against us, unraveling the very fabric of our love with a cruel twist of fate.

I could still see the way Dina had smiled at me, the way her laughter had danced through the air like a melody that could brighten even the darkest of days. I had taken that for granted, convinced that the future we envisioned together was a certainty, something I could hold on to without fear. But now, that future had slipped away like sand through my fingers, leaving behind only a barren landscape of regret and sorrow.

Aeon stepped back, her face pale and drawn, the lines of worry etched into her brow like a map of my anguish. "I'll give you some time," she murmured, her voice barely above a whisper. As she retreated into the shadows, I felt an odd mixture of relief and anger wash over me. Relief that I could be alone with my thoughts.

But even in her absence, the darkness enveloped me, thick and suffocating, pressing in on all sides as if to remind me of the weight of my reality. I was left alone with my thoughts, trapped in a void that felt all-consuming, a deep chasm that echoed with the silence of a love unfulfilled. The walls around me seemed to close in tighter, the air thick with the taste of despair that clung to my tongue like ashes.

The reality of my loss loomed over me, an insurmountable wall that threatened to crush me beneath its weight. Every breath felt labored, as if I were struggling against an invisible force, and each passing moment became a reminder of the inevitable void Dina would leave behind. I had let my desires lead me astray, blinded by the thrill of newfound attention and the allure of something forbidden. I had taken for granted the one person who mattered most in my life—the woman who had stood by me through every storm, the one who had made my heart feel whole.

Now, as I sat there in the oppressive silence, the truth settled heavily upon my chest: I had betrayed her in my heart, flirting with the idea of happiness elsewhere while she was fighting for her life. Guilt washed over me like a tidal wave, drowning out any remnants of the fleeting pleasure I had sought.

And now, in the silence that followed, all I could do was sit with my grief, the echoes of a love lost reverberating through me like a haunting melody, each note a reminder of the laughter we would never share again, the dreams we would never pursue. The future I had imagined—filled with joy and love—now felt like a cruel illusion, a mirage that had vanished into thin air. I was left with nothing but the bitter taste of regret, the realization that I had squandered the most precious gift life had given me.

The emptiness settled in, wrapping around me like a shroud, isolating me from the world outside. All the hopes and dreams I had harbored now felt like distant stars, flickering in a night sky I could no longer reach. I was anchored in this moment of despair, each thought a reminder of what could have been, the potential of a love that would never flourish. The silence grew heavier, enveloping me in a cocoon of sorrow as I faced the darkest truth of all: without Dina, I was adrift, lost in a sea of unfulfilled dreams and haunting memories.

Chapter 15

The sky was overcast, a dull, heavy gray that felt like it was pressing down on my chest. I hated it. Hated how it seemed to mock the emptiness inside me, as if even the sun couldn't be bothered to shine today. Inside the funeral hall, everything was muted—the hushed voices, the gentle rustle of black clothing, the soft scent of flowers that couldn't mask the overwhelming smell of grief.

I sat in a corner, trying to disappear. I didn't want to talk to anyone, didn't want to see the pity in their eyes, or hear the same words of comfort they'd been repeating all day. What did they know about comfort? About loss? They could go home tonight, back to their families, back to normalcy. I was the one who had to wake up tomorrow without Dina.

I glanced over at the small, polished urn on the altar, and my heart clenched. That was all that was left of her. Everything she was, everything we'd been, reduced to ashes inside that tiny, delicate container. It was like a cruel joke—something so monumental, so life-altering, reduced to something you could hold in one hand. I had to keep reminding myself that this wasn't some nightmare I'd wake up from. Dina was gone, and there was nothing I could do to bring her back.

I barely noticed when Dina's mom came up to me. She sat down beside me, and for a second, I thought about standing up and walking away, but my legs felt too heavy to move. She placed a hand on my shoulder, and I didn't look at her, just kept staring at the floor.

"She loved you, Jack," she said softly, her voice gentle but firm, like she was trying to make sure I understood. "She always told me how much she admired your strength. How she felt safe when you were around."

I couldn't hold it back anymore. I broke. Tears started pouring down my face, and I didn't even care who saw. I just clung to her hand, the way a drowning man clings to anything that might keep him afloat. She didn't say anything else, just held me, letting me cry until I felt like I had nothing left inside me.

When I finally managed to pull myself together, she gave me a small, sad smile. "Would you like to say a few words, in memory of Dina?" she asked, her eyes soft but insistent. "I think she would have wanted that."

I didn't want to. God, I didn't want to. But I nodded anyway. I owed it to Dina, didn't I? So I stood up, even though my legs felt like they could barely hold me, and slowly walked to the front of the room. Everyone was watching, waiting for me to say something, but the words wouldn't come. I opened my mouth, but it was like my throat had closed up. I just stood there, staring at nothing, feeling every pair of eyes on me.

Then I saw it. The piano. It was just off to the side, sleek and polished, like it had been waiting for me this whole time. I don't know what made me move, but I walked over and sat down on the bench, my hands hovering over the keys. I didn't even know how to play, but it felt... right, somehow, to be here.

As I sat there, I closed my eyes, and then it hit me — like a punch to the gut.

I came home late one night, tired from work and just wanting to crash on the couch. But when I walked into the living room, there was Dina, sitting in her wheelchair, staring at her laptop with tears streaming down her cheeks.

"Hey," I said, my heart skipping a beat. "What's wrong? Why are you crying?"

She looked up at me, and there was this sad, beautiful smile on her face. "The Itchyworms released a new music video," she said, wiping her tears but still smiling. "It's... it's just really beautiful, Jack. It got to me."

I couldn't help but laugh a little. "So you're crying because of a music video?" I teased, even though I could see how serious she was.

She nodded, her smile not wavering. "Yeah. It sounds silly, but... if I ever —" She hesitated, her eyes dropping to her lap before she continued. "If I ever die, I'd want someone to sing this song at my funeral."

I remember laughing, brushing it off. "Come on, don't talk like that. You're not going anywhere. And by the time we're old and wrinkly, I won't even remember this conversation."

She laughed, too, and for a moment, everything felt light again. We let the music play, and I thought nothing more of it.

I opened my eyes, and for a second, I could almost see her there, sitting beside me, smiling that same sad, beautiful smile. I didn't think. I just... started playing. At first, I fumbled over the keys, trying to find the right notes, but as my hands moved, it was like something took over. Like Dina was guiding me, showing me where to go.

The first notes were shaky, almost fragile, like I was afraid they'd break. I hesitated, but then I could feel her, like a warm presence just behind me, her hands lightly over mine, steadying them. And I kept playing. I closed my eyes, letting the melody lead me, letting it all spill out, the way I should have done so many times before.

I started singing "Di Na Muli," my voice rough, cracking under the weight of everything I was feeling. I could barely get the words out at first, but I kept going, even though it hurt. I sang like it was the last thing I'd ever do, like every word was for her, and her alone.

As I sang, the memories started flooding back—her laugh, bright and clear, echoing through our tiny home; the way she'd reach for my hand, even when she was tired or in pain; the way she looked at me at the hospital while I was recovering, when she made me promise to be strong. Like she knew, somehow, that I'd be standing here, singing this song for her.

I thought of all the times I should have been there for her but wasn't. All the times I let work, or my stupid pride, get in the way. Every time I chose something else over just sitting with her, holding her hand, talking to her. And now, it was too late. There was no going back, no more chances to make it right.

The room was silent, except for the piano and my voice, and I just kept my eyes closed, letting the song carry me. I wasn't playing for anyone else. I was playing for Dina. For everything I wished I'd said. For everything I never got to tell her. For all the love I had, that I didn't know how to show until it was too late.

Each word felt like it was tearing something out of me, leaving me raw and exposed. But I didn't stop, even when it hurt. Especially when it hurt. I needed to feel this, to let myself feel every bit of it, because it was all I had left of her.

As I hit the last note, I let it linger, as if holding on to the last thread of a dream before waking up. And then... silence. I just sat there, my hands shaking, my chest tight, my eyes blurry with tears. I looked down at my hands, at the keys, trying to understand how I had just done that. It felt like she was there, like she had been playing through me, and now she was gone again, leaving me with nothing but the ache where she used to be.

I lifted my head, and that's when I saw them—everyone in the room, staring at me. Some were crying, quietly wiping their faces, others just looked... stunned. Like they couldn't believe what they'd just heard. Like I had somehow managed to say everything they were feeling but couldn't express.

And for a moment, I felt something shift. Like maybe, through the music, I had given them a piece of her. A piece of the love we shared, the love that I never quite knew how to show until now. But it didn't make the emptiness go away. If anything, it made it sharper, clearer, because I knew I could never play it for her again.

I glanced at her urn, sitting there, surrounded by flowers, and it felt like my heart was being squeezed in a fist. I wanted to believe she could hear me, that somehow, she was still there, smiling that same sad, beautiful smile. But I didn't know. And that not knowing... it was going to break me.

I didn't know what to do. I felt like I was going to suffocate, so I just ran. I pushed through the doors and out into the cold air, trying to breathe, trying to stop the ache in my chest.

I barely heard Angga's footsteps behind me, but there she was, her heels clicking softly on the floor, cutting through the muffled sounds of grief around us. She slipped into my line of sight, a picture of calm, with that small, businesslike smile on her lips, like this was just another day at the office. "That was beautiful, Jack," she said, her voice smooth, almost gentle, like she was offering condolences. But I could see it, the way her eyes gleamed—a predator sensing an opportunity. "Really... touching. We should record it. Release it as a single."

I stared at her, trying to process the words, trying to understand if I'd heard her right. She was still talking, her tone professional, like she was discussing sales figures, not the song I'd just played for my dead wife. "My wife just died," I said, my voice low, barely steady. "Leave me alone."

Angga's smile didn't waver. She didn't even flinch. If anything, she seemed to lean in closer, like a snake coiling around its prey. "I know, Jack. I'm truly sorry for your loss." She spoke slowly, carefully, as if she was choosing her words to avoid triggering an alarm. "But you have to see the bigger picture here. That performance... it was raw. Honest. It's something people are going to feel. It could touch millions. Think about what it could do for your career, for the band."

"Stop." The word came out louder than I meant, a desperate, jagged edge to it. I could see her eyes widen, just a little, but the cool, calculating glint didn't fade. "You're cold-blooded, you know that? I quit. I'm done."

She tilted her head slightly, as if she was surprised, as if she hadn't expected me to push back. But the smile stayed, patient, patronizing. "Fine," she said, a hint of amusement slipping into her voice. "If that's how you feel, Jack. But let's be clear—you're just one part of this band. Jay, Aeon... they understand what's at stake. They can take care of it." Her hand dipped into her pocket, and she pulled out her phone, waving it slightly. "I already got most of the performance recorded. We can still make it work. Even without you."

I could feel my stomach twist, a sick, cold feeling spreading through me. She had been recording? At Dina's funeral? I didn't even have the energy to be angry, to shout or argue. I was just... tired. I looked at her, really looked at her, and all I saw was a mask. Polished, professional, and utterly heartless.

"Do whatever you want," I said, my voice barely above a whisper. I felt like I was choking on the words, but I forced them out anyway. "Just... leave me alone."

Angga's smile sharpened, and for a moment, I thought I saw something dark flicker across her face, a hint of triumph. "Of course, Jack. I'll give you some space. But remember... this is bigger than you. And whether you're in or out, the world's going to hear that song. You can't stop that."

She turned and walked away, her heels clicking softly, leaving me standing there, feeling like I was sinking, like the ground had dropped out from under me. The music, the band, everything... it felt so small, so meaningless compared to the empty, gaping hole Dina left behind. And all I could do was watch as Angga disappeared into the crowd, already planning her next move, like she hadn't even heard the song, like it hadn't meant anything to her at all.

I turned my back on Angga, leaving her standing there, a calculating smile on her lips as she plotted her next move. The day was winding down, and a profound heaviness settled on my shoulders.

I felt a desperate urge to escape, to find a dark corner of the world where I could drown my sorrows in alcohol until I couldn't feel anything at all.

The bar beckoned like a siren's call, a sanctuary where the pain of loss might be muted, even if just for a little while. I longed for the cold embrace of liquor to wash over me, to dissolve the sharp edges of grief that threatened to slice through my heart. Every step away from Angga was a step closer to finding solace, a momentary reprieve from the suffocating weight of my reality.

As I moved through the thinning crowd, I could almost taste the bitter tang of beer on my lips. The noise of the funeral faded, replaced by the promise of numbing oblivion. I was more than ready to dive into the depths of the bar, to let the darkness envelop me, to silence the ache that clung to me like a shadow, reminding me of everything I had lost.

Chapter 16

I sat slumped over the bar, nursing my guilt with another bottle of beer, barely tasting it as I drank. The dim lights above flickered, and the television buzzed behind the counter. The news was celebrating the sold-out concert of the new Itchyworms. They'd played just two days ago, and there were Aeon and Jay—playing the piano and drums, respectively—and some new guitarist had taken my place. Laya, the new lead singer, performed "Hindi Na Mauulit," now the top song in Asia. The band's success stung, like a wound freshly reopened.

"Even the title's wrong," I muttered under my breath, bitterness spilling over. "Should be 'Di Na Muli,' scumbags!" The words came out sharper than I intended. Then a figure slid onto the stool next to me. I squinted, trying to make out his face through the fog of alcohol and regret. There was something oddly familiar about him, but I couldn't quite place it.

"Care for a story?" he asked, his voice soft but somehow unnerving.

I waved my hand, not really caring. "Whatever," I slurred, resting my head against the bar's cool surface.

"Once upon a time, there was a man who was deeply in love with his college friend," the stranger began, his tone taking on a wistful, almost nostalgic quality. "He wanted nothing more than to tell her how he felt, but he never did. He waited, clinging to the hope she'd notice him one day. Then, she approached him about auditioning for their college band, and he thought it was his chance. They'd finally be close, share something special. He imagined that maybe she'd see him differently."

As he spoke, his gaze drifted, like he was watching scenes play out in front of him. "But she was already in love with someone else," he said, his voice growing softer, almost bitter. "Someone who had her heart without even trying. No matter what he did, he stayed a shadow, always on the sidelines, watching her laugh and smile with the one who didn't even have to try."

A chill crept over me as he went on. "For years, he played his part as her friend, hoping that one day things would change. But they didn't. She was happiest with the other man, completely unaware of the one who stayed quietly by her side, suffering in silence."

The stranger's voice turned darker. "Time went by, and the college band thrived. They shared stages and memories, but he remained invisible. Just a side character in her life story. And then, one day, he saw her smile fade as her love turned his attention to someone else. Desperate to bring her happiness back, he became convinced he'd do anything for her—even if it meant drastic measures."

The words sank in, clawing at memories buried deep within me—memories of the stage, of faces I'd tried to forget. It felt disturbingly familiar, but I couldn't quite piece it together through the haze of alcohol.

"Then came a show," the man continued, his voice lowering, "and the other man brought his wife along. When the girl saw them, her whole world shattered. She tried to hide it, but he could see right through her. That was the moment he decided to give her back the happiness she'd lost—even if it meant destroying someone else."

My stomach twisted as he spoke, each word pressing down on me like a weight. "The man found the other man's wife backstage and told her he needed to talk to her privately. She trusted him—why wouldn't she? She didn't know she was walking into a trap."

He leaned closer, voice barely a whisper. "He locked the door behind her and set the venue ablaze. He thought she'd die and his friend would be free to love again. But she survived, though barely. She was left crippled, her life changed forever. And as the other man pulled away from her in despair, the girl found herself smiling again, if only for a brief moment."

A wave of nausea hit me. I gripped the edge of the bar, heart pounding as if it could escape my chest. The story was clawing its way into my head, and I couldn't escape the feeling that I knew exactly where this was going.

"Eventually," the stranger said, "the other man regained his fame, and the girl found the courage to declare her feelings. But he rejected her, still loyal to his wife despite everything. That's when the man made his choice: he'd finish what he started."

I looked up, feeling the words hit me like a blow to the gut. "You're—"

But he cut me off, his voice low and chilling. "This is just a story...or is it?" He paused, his eyes locking onto mine with a knowing look, and suddenly, everything fell into place. Memories rushed back—conversations, glances, betrayals. My heart pounded as I realized who he was.

"You...Jay?"

Before I could move, he slipped a knife from his jacket. "Goodbye, Jack."

"Wait—" I barely got the word out before he drove the blade into my side, the cold metal slicing through flesh. I gasped, the pain overwhelming, and collapsed to the floor. I looked up, seeing his face, the face of someone I once trusted. The betrayal hit harder than the pain.

As my vision darkened, his silhouette became blurry, and I heard a voice, not his, but something else, echoing through the darkness, soft but powerful.

"Have you chosen well?"

Chapter 17

The air felt thick and charged with an otherworldly energy as I found myself standing in Mayari's domain once more. The landscape shimmered with a surreal light, colors swirling like thoughts in a chaotic mind. It was both familiar and unsettling, a haunting reminder of the choices I had made and the paths I had walked. The colors twisted, vibrant and chaotic, like a storm brewing behind closed eyes, threatening to burst and consume everything in its wake.

"Why did my alternate life end like that?" I called out, the words tumbling from my lips before I could hold them back. "You said no one would die. Why did it have to happen this way?"

Mayari emerged, her presence both comforting and intimidating. Her eyes, deep and knowing, seemed to pierce through the facade I had built around myself. "Indeed, the price was only the existence of the Itchyworms," she began, her voice echoing like a distant melody. "But your choices stirred the wheel of fate. Your fame and fortune came at a cost—Dina's life, your sorrow, and ultimately, your own death."

I clenched my fists, feeling the weight of her words. Each syllable felt like a stone dropping into the well of my conscience, sending ripples of regret through my thoughts. Memories of past moments flashed through my mind: Dina's bright smile the first time we met, her eyes lighting up when she talked about her dreams. How she trusted me, how she believed in us. And then, that fateful day when everything changed—when she was left in that wheelchair because of choices I made. I could still hear her screams, see the confusion and pain in her eyes as she lay there, broken, because I couldn't protect her.

"But what about Jay's attempted killing of Dina at the gig? Was that true in the real world?" My voice cracked as I spoke, afraid of the answer I already suspected.

"Yes," she replied, her tone unwavering. "That was a consequence of your negligence. If only you had straightened things out with Aeon—if you had been honest with her about your feelings, rather than flirting with her, then perhaps she wouldn't have remained vulnerable to Jay's delusions."

A wave of guilt washed over me, heavier than any burden I had ever carried. I had been a fool, dancing around my emotions while everyone else suffered. I remembered those times with Aeon, when I'd see her watching me from across the room, her eyes hopeful yet uncertain. I could have been clear with her, but I played with her feelings, thinking it was harmless.

"So, it's my fault," I murmured, the bitterness of regret coating my words. "If I had just been honest..." My voice was barely above a whisper now, each word feeling like it was being dragged out from the pit of my gut.

"Exactly," Mayari interrupted, her gaze unyielding. "You were the catalyst in this tragic story. Your indecision allowed Jay to spiral into madness. And in his madness, he acted on the darkness in his heart."

I felt my knees weaken as the reality of her words settled in. My mind raced through the chaos of memories, trying to find something, anything, that would make her wrong. I remembered laughing with Jay over drinks, talking about our dreams and ambitions, never realizing how deep his resentment went. Had I really been so blind? Was I caught up in my own world that I didn't see the danger right in front of me?

"What can I do?" I pleaded, desperation creeping into my voice. "I want to fix this—I want a do-over."

Mayari shook her head, a sorrowful expression crossing her face. "No, Jack. That alternate earth will move forward without you. It is a world shaped by your choices, and you cannot rewrite the past."

Her words felt like a death sentence. I wanted to scream, to cry, to beg for another chance, but the truth was, I didn't deserve one. I had made my choices, and now, those choices had carved a path I couldn't stray from. Dina's lifeless eyes, Aeon's broken spirit, Jay's twisted smile—all of them haunted me, and there was no escape.

"But what am I supposed to do now?" I asked, feeling the hope drain from my voice. The void of possibility loomed around me, threatening to swallow me whole. The landscape seemed to darken, the swirling lights now dull and cold, like a sky heavy with storm clouds, ready to burst. I was drowning, and I couldn't see a way out.

"There are two options," she said, her tone steady, yet heavy with meaning. Her words seemed to echo, reverberating through the empty expanse around us, as if the universe itself was holding its breath, waiting for my decision. "You can return to the real world, where waking up is nearly impossible, a place where your body is trapped in a silent struggle against oblivion. If you choose this, you will linger on the edge of consciousness, a heartbeat away from vanishing, fighting a battle you may never win. Or," she paused, her gaze darkening, "you can wait here, within this void, until the Deity of the afterlife comes to guide you to your final resting place."

The air felt colder, sharper, as she spoke. Each word was like a chisel, carving out the reality of my situation. I could almost see the two paths forming before me—one shrouded in shadows, endless and uncertain, and the other stretching out like a long, dark tunnel with a distant, dim light at the end. My chest tightened, and I realized I was holding my breath, afraid to let it out because it felt like admitting defeat.

Her voice softened, but it was still laced with an inevitability that made my skin crawl. "There is no third option to undo the past, Jack. The life you knew, the choices you made, they have already shaped the course of that world. You cannot rewind time, nor can you erase the consequences of your actions."

The finality of her words hung in the air like a dark cloud, and I could feel despair creeping back in, cold and suffocating. My heart sank, the weight of everything crushing down, as if the very world beneath my feet was slipping away. It felt like being trapped at the bottom of an ocean, every breath a struggle, every thought suffused with the futility of escape.

Just when I thought I was alone in my misery, drowning in the hopelessness of it all, a voice cut through the silence—a familiar, taunting whisper that sent chills down my spine. It was low, smooth, like the hiss of a snake, slithering into the space between us.

"No, Mayari," the voice said, calm yet sinister, "there is always another choice."

I turned, and from the shadows, Angga's figure materialized, dark and enigmatic, her eyes gleaming with a dangerous light. She stepped forward, her presence like a ripple through the fabric of the realm, unsettling and yet undeniable. Her lips curled into a smirk, a promise of something twisted, something that could shatter the fragile balance Mayari had laid before me.

"Jack," she continued, her tone dripping with a mix of allure and malice, "this is the other option. Get revenge."

Chapter 18

"Angga?" I whispered, my voice barely more than a rasp.

Before Angga could reply to me, Mayari asked her, what are you doing here?

Angga's smirk grew, and before I could blink, her form began to shift. The lithe, dark figure morphed, growing taller, muscles expanding beneath her skin. The delicate femininity gave way to a more commanding, masculine presence, yet there was still a strange, graceful beauty to it. When the transformation finished, the person standing before us was not Angga at all, but a powerful, almost ethereal being—an imposing figure with a chiseled frame, dark eyes that held ancient wisdom, and an aura that sent shivers down my spine.

"I am Sidapa," he declared, his voice deeper, yet still feminine.. "The deity of death."

I felt a chill run through my veins. Sidapa. The name echoed like a ghostly whisper in the silence that followed. I had heard of him, of course—the god who presided over the end of life, the one who guided souls to their final rest. But to see him here, in Mayari's domain, was beyond anything I could have imagined.

Mayari's shock was quickly replaced by a calm, steely composure. "What are you doing here, Sidapa," she said, but there was a note of unease in her voice. "You are not yet needed here."

Perhaps. Yet my curiosity has been stirred, drawn to this mortal you have taken such interest in.

He turned his gaze to me, and I felt like he was peeling away every layer, every defense I had left. "I was waiting for you, Jack," he said, his tone almost mocking. "Your soul was supposed to cross into my domain right after your motorcycle met that truck many moons ago. But you never arrived. I wondered, what could possibly delay the inevitable? And then I saw her," he said, nodding towards Mayari. "Meddling."

"Meddling?" I repeated, my voice weak, trying to process everything. "What do you mean?"

Sidapa's eyes glinted with amusement. "Mayari has sent you to another world instead . It was... an interesting choice, to say the least. A deity tampering with fate for the sake of a mortal." He glanced at Mayari, a sardonic smile playing on his lips. "I couldn't fathom why she would do this for you, Jack. But it intrigued me. So, I decided to follow."

What are you saying?" I asked, the confusion bubbling into anger. "You... you followed me? Why?"

Sidapa stepped closer, his presence overwhelming, almost suffocating. "I took an interest in your story, Jack. I wanted to understand what made you so significant that even a goddess would bend the rules for you. So, I took on a form—a guise, if you will. Angga became my vessel, through whom I could observe, guide, and wait for this moment."

Mayari's face hardened, her voice cold as steel. "This was never your right to take," she said sharply. "It was my choice alone."

"Oh, but I did," Sidapa countered, his smile vanishing. "You see, Mayari, every soul belongs to me eventually. And I found your little experiment fascinating. I saw Jack's life unravel, saw the chaos and the choices that led to this moment. And I began to see something... familiar."

Sidapa's gaze softened, and for a moment, the air around him seemed less cold, less sharp. "I saw Aeon," he said quietly. "Her unrequited love for Jack. It reminded me of... myself."

I blinked, caught off guard. "What do you mean?"

I watched him, trying to understand. It was as if he was lost in his own thoughts, his eyes distant, staring at something far beyond this place. Then, with a slow, deliberate motion, Sidapa raised his hand, and the shadows around us began to stir, twisting and coiling like dark tendrils. They shifted and merged, forming vague shapes that gradually sharpened into figures—a spectral play unfolding before my eyes.

"Long ago," Sidapa began, his voice low and resonant, "I loved another god. Bulan, the deity of the moon." As he spoke, the shadows molded into the form of a luminous figure, delicate and radiant, bathed in soft, silvery light. The image of Bulan appeared, his face serene, his eyes distant, like a dream come to life. "He was beautiful, radiant, everything I could never be."

The shadowy Bulan stood beneath a moonlit sky, his ethereal glow a stark contrast to the darkness surrounding him. I could almost see the light caress his skin, reflecting off him like water. "But our love was forbidden," Sidapa continued, his voice carrying a weight that felt ancient, like a lament that had echoed through centuries. "A secret that could never see the light."

As Sidapa's words echoed, the shadows shifted again, revealing a second figure—darker, taller, a silhouette that loomed in the background, always at the edge of the light, watching but never able to step forward. "We were both gods, both male, and the heavens did not smile upon our union." The shadow of Sidapa lingered in the dark, close enough to touch but never able to reach the radiant figure of Bulan, who stood bathed in moonlight, serene and untouchable.

I glanced at Mayari, but her face remained unreadable, her eyes fixed on the shadows as if she was trying to suppress something within herself.

"Bulan was everything to me," Sidapa said, and his voice softened, carrying an ache that felt timeless. "But in the end, he chose her." The shadows shifted once more, and the image of Bulan turned, his face lifting toward another figure—Mayari, her form ethereal and glowing. The two figures drew closer, their hands almost touching, and the dark silhouette of Sidapa remained behind, retreating further into the shadows.

"He married Mayari, the goddess of the moon," Sidapa's voice was quieter now, but the bitterness in his tone was sharp enough to cut through the air. "And I was left with nothing but my own grief." The shadows darkened, and the image of Bulan and Mayari standing together grew clearer, brighter, as if to emphasize the distance between them and the dark, solitary figure that lingered at the edge of the scene.

"I watched them from afar, watched as they shared a love that should have been mine." The shadow of Sidapa drifted further back, shrinking until it seemed like nothing more than a speck of darkness against the bright, glowing figures. "And so, I buried my love deep inside, letting it fester, letting it turn to something dark."

The shadows seemed to tremble, as if they were alive, and I could feel the intensity of his words, the way they seemed to fill the space around us, making it hard to breathe. The bright figures of Bulan and Mayari faded, leaving only the shadow of Sidapa, now larger, looming over everything, a dark cloud that swallowed the light.

"You see, Jack," Sidapa said, and the shadows around us began to recede, his voice growing clearer, more resolute. "I recognized that same longing in Aeon—the longing for someone who would never truly be hers. And maybe that's why I decided to stay, to watch over your little drama. To see how it would end. Because in her, I saw myself. And in you, I saw... an opportunity."

"Opportunity?" I echoed, a sinking feeling growing in my stomach.

Sidapa's smile returned, colder this time. "Yes. You were Mayari's plaything, her experiment. And I thought, why not make things a bit more interesting? Why not push the story in a direction she never intended?" He stepped closer, until he was standing right in front of me, his eyes boring into mine. "She was already done with her toy so she is discarding it already, but I offer you another opportunity to renew your story. Which brings us to my option, Revenge."

"I am giving you another chance, Jack," Sidapa continued, his tone measured yet unyielding. "You will wake up in the real world, alive, but not in the body you once knew. Your original form lies in a hospital bed, caught between life and death, and your time to reclaim it is limited. You will have only until the moon reaches its zenith tonight to fulfill two conditions and return to your own skin. Fail, and your soul will drift, forever untethered from the life you so desperately cling to."

I felt my pulse quicken, the weight of his words sinking in.

"First," Sidapa said, his eyes narrowing, "you must sever Aeon's obsession with you. You must be clear, make her understand that her love is unreturned. This is to cleanse your mind of lingering guilt, the burden of false hope you've allowed to grow. And second..." His voice dropped, almost to a whisper, his words like a dark current slipping through the air. "You must make Jay pay. He crippled Dina, he was the instrument of your chaos, and he will not escape the consequences. You must seek out vengeance. This act is to cleanse your heart of the rage that has poisoned it, the anger you've let fester without release."

I opened my mouth to speak, but he raised a hand, silencing me. "And one more thing, Jack. While you walk in this borrowed skin, you will not speak to Dina. You will not reveal yourself to her, nor attempt to explain your true identity. To do so would risk complicating everything—her fragile hope, your mission, the very threads that hold this reality together. She must not see you as you are, not until your tasks are complete."

I wanted to protest, to ask why I couldn't see her, even just once. But Sidapa's gaze pinned me down, making it clear that there was no room for negotiation. "If you wish to return to your life, to her, you must follow these rules. There is no other way."

I glanced at Mayari, searching for a sign, a reason to refuse. But there was only silence, her face unreadable, her eyes unfathomable.

"What will you choose, Jack?" Sidapa asked, his voice like a whisper, like the darkness at the edge of a dream. "Will you stay here, or will you take the path I am offering?"

I swallowed, my mind a storm of fear, confusion, and hope. It felt like every decision I had ever made had led to this moment, and I was terrified of making the wrong one. But as I looked at Sidapa, I realized that this was not just about me. This was about Dina, about Aeon, about all the lives I had touched and broken.

"I'll do it," I said, my voice barely more than a whisper. "I'll fulfill your conditions."

Sidapa smiled, but there was no warmth in it. "Good. Then let's begin."

Chapter 19

S idapa smiled, but there was no warmth in it. "Good. Then let's begin."

His smile felt more like a warning than an invitation. He blew a kiss into the air, and before I could react, I felt myself falling.

The world blurred into a cacophony of colors and sounds, a sensation of weightlessness engulfing me. I fell for what felt like an eternity, the air rushing past until, with a sudden jolt, everything went dark.

When I opened my eyes, harsh fluorescent lights burned down on me. My body felt heavy, unresponsive. Panic surged as I realized I was lying on a cold steel table in a morgue. Nausea rolled through me, and I forced myself to sit up, only to be met with a chilling reality—my body was lifeless. No pulse, no heartbeat, no breath escaping my lips. I was trapped in a shell that had already succumbed to death.

"What the hell?" I muttered, my voice sounding strangely muted, like a whisper echoing in a void. I swung my legs over the side of the table and stood, my feet hitting the cold floor with a dull thud.

Just then, the door swung open, and a morgue attendant stepped in, clipboard in hand. Their eyes widened, mouth agape, then they dropped the clipboard with a loud clatter.

"What in the—?" they stammered, backing away.

"Hey, hey! It's okay! I'm not here to cause any trouble!" I called out, raising my hands in a gesture of peace. My body, however, seemed intent on chaos, and I stumbled forward, arms flailing as I tried to regain my balance.

The attendant turned and fled, shouting, "There's a live one in here! Call the cops!"

I couldn't help but chuckle at the absurdity of the situation. "What, can't a guy just wake up in a morgue without causing a scene?" I called after them, shaking my head.

But that comic relief didn't help the gravity of my situation. I glanced around the sterile room, looking for something—any-thing—that could help me understand what was happening. A clock on the wall ticked loudly, each second echoing in my mind like a countdown. I approached it and saw the time: just under twelve hours until midnight.

"Great," I muttered, running a hand through my hair—or what felt like my hair. I needed a plan—fast. I had two conditions to fulfill to reclaim my old life, but urgency clouded my thoughts.

Pacing the small room, my mind raced with ideas that crashed and burned one after another. Severing Aeon's obsession and getting revenge on Jay felt monumental, especially since I was in the body of someone who had just died.

Before I could sort through the chaos, the door creaked open again. This time, it was a woman in a police uniform, her expression a mix of confusion and concern.

"Enzo?" she called, peering into the room.

My breath caught in my throat. Enzo? That was the name of the body I inhabited. I quickly glanced in the mirror, and a face I didn't recognize stared back at me — striking, with sharp features and dark hair, but ultimately just a shell.

"Uh, yeah, that's me!" I blurted, panic rising in my chest.

The woman stepped inside, her gaze darting between me and the body on the table. "How are you alive?" she demanded, crossing her arms, skepticism written all over her face.

"Uh... long story," I stammered, trying to keep my composure. "I—I'm not actually Enzo. I mean, I'm in his body, but I'm not—"

"Not Enzo?" She raised an eyebrow, disbelief evident. "You're telling me you're a spirit or something?"

"More like a guy who just got back from the afterlife and didn't get the welcome mat," I quipped, attempting a weak smile.

"Cut the crap," she snapped, her expression hardening. "You're not making any sense. Who are you?"

I took a deep breath, knowing I needed to be honest, yet unsure how to convey the truth without sounding completely insane. "Look, I know this sounds crazy, but I was in this other world, and now I'm in Enzo's body. I have twelve hours to, uh, fix some things before... well, before I'm trapped for good."

The woman's eyes narrowed as she processed my words, skepticism battling curiosity. "So you expect me to believe you're some kind of... ghost?"

"It's not just a ghost thing! I swear, I can prove it!" I exclaimed, desperation creeping into my voice.

She stepped closer, her fingers brushing against Enzo's arm, feeling the coldness of his skin. "This isn't right," she murmured, glancing back at the body on the table. "He's... gone. There's no warmth left in him."

I nodded, the gravity of the situation weighing heavily on me. "Exactly. I'm not him. I mean, I'm in his body, but I'm not him. His soul is gone."

Rica—at least, I assumed that was her name from the badge—studied me, her expression a mix of disbelief and concern. "So, if you're not Enzo, then who are you?"

"Jack," I said, the name slipping from my lips like a lifeline. "And I need your help."

Her gaze flicked back to Enzo's body. "You're really telling me the truth?"

"I swear it," I insisted, urgency driving my words. "But there's more. I need to get to my real body, and—"

"Your real body?" she interrupted, skepticism creeping back into her voice. "You think I'm just going to believe all of this?"

"Look, I don't have time for this," I urged. "If you don't believe me, then just leave me alone."

I started walking toward the door and stepped past her, exiting the morgue. I felt her eyes on my back, skepticism still lingering in her expression while she followed me. I could hardly blame her; I was living a nightmare that seemed impossible to explain.

As we traversed the hospital, I caught a glimpse of my original body, lying in a hospital bed, with Dina sleeping at the side. My heart—or whatever was left of it—twisted painfully in my chest. I wanted to call out to her, to reach out, but Sidapa's condition loomed over me like a shadow. I couldn't break that promise.

"Hey!" Rica's voice snapped me back to reality.

I turned to her, swallowing hard. "That's my body over there," I said, pointing. "And the girl next to it is my wife, Dina."

Rica's gaze shifted to the sleeping figure, and for the first time, I saw a flicker of empathy in her eyes. "Look... I—"

Before she could finish, I interrupted, urgency creeping into my voice. "Ask her questions only I would know. I promise, our answers will be the same."

Rica hesitated, her brow furrowing as she contemplated the situation. "Okay, but I need to make sure this isn't some sort of trick."

"Just wake her up and ask," I urged. "I'll be waiting around the corner. Make it quick; I'm pressed for time. Try to ask about the flavor of ice cream I was buying before the accident."

Rica approached Dina, her expression shifting to one of professional determination. She gently shook Dina's shoulder. "Ma'am? I need you to wake up."

Dina stirred, her eyes fluttering open to the dim light of the hospital room. Confusion washed over her face as she noticed Rica standing there. "What's going on?" she asked, her voice thick with sleep.

"Ma'am, I'm Officer Rica," she said, her tone professional yet gentle. "I'm investigating the accident involving your husband. I need to ask you a few questions to help with the case."

Dina blinked, a shadow of concern washing over her face as her gaze drifted toward the bed where my body lay still and lifeless. "Jack..." she whispered, her voice barely audible.

Rica paused, her expression empathetic but firm. "I can't discuss details right now. I just need you to answer a few questions about him, alright? It's important."

Dina's brow furrowed, her heart pounding as she nodded, still visibly shaken. "Okay, I'll do my best."

"Thank you," Rica said, maintaining her professional demeanor. "Can you tell me what Jack was doing right before the accident?"

Dina hesitated, her expression clouded with sorrow. "He told me he was drinking with his buddies from work..."

"Alright," Rica continued, jotting down notes. "There was a mention of ice cream. Can you tell me something about that?"

Dina's eyes brightened momentarily as she recalled, "He bought me a tub of vanilla, which is my second favorite flavor after mango ube delight."

"Thanks," Rica said, her tone remaining focused. "That's all for now. I appreciate your cooperation."

After thanking Dina, Rica stepped outside, where I waited in the shadows, anxious and hopeful.

"What did she say?" I asked, eager for any progress.

Rica locked eyes with me, still trying to understand. "You actually bought her a tub of chocolate ice cream?"

I shook my head, noticing her intentional mix-up with the flavor. "No, it was a tub of vanilla. I wanted mango ube delight, but someone else had already snatched up the last one. That woman ended up being one of the deities who put me in this mess."

Rica raised an eyebrow, skepticism evident in her expression. "Are you really asking me to believe that a deity is buying ice cream in the middle of the night?"

I ran a hand through my hair, frustration bubbling up. "Look, it's either you believe me or not. But I need to accomplish these tasks."

Rica crossed her arms, her disbelief mingling with curiosity. "I can't just overlook what you're saying. This is... unbelievable."

I took a deep breath, steeling myself. "I know it sounds crazy, but if you still don't believe me, it's up to you. I must go now and think of a plan."

Rica's expression shifted as the weight of my words sank in. "Okay, fine, let me help you," she finally said, her voice steady. "But on one condition: Tell me everything, every detail. I need to understand what's happening here."

I took a moment to gather my thoughts, knowing that every piece of information could be vital. As I explained my situation—how Sidapa had given me two tasks to complete so I could return to my real body—the urgency pressed down on us like a heavy weight. For the first time, I felt a flicker of hope. With Rica's help, maybe I could confront my challenges and reclaim my life.

Rica furrowed her brow after hearing my story, silenced for a moment before speaking what was on her mind. "Jack, after this, I also need your help."

"What's that?" I asked, my heart racing at the prospect of her support.

"I want to talk to this Sidapa," she insisted, her voice firm. "Maybe if I talk to him, he would also bring back Enzo's soul."

I sighed, feeling the weight of her request. "I can't promise anything. I don't have that kind of authority, and I don't know if Sidapa will want to speak with you."

Rica crossed her arms, determination etched on her face. "Then you'll have to try, Jack."

"Deal," I said, relief flooding through me—I wasn't alone in this after all. "Let's figure out a plan."

We huddled close, urgency propelling us forward. As I met Rica's gaze, a spark of hope ignited within me. Maybe—just maybe—I could navigate this chaos with her help.

The clock was ticking.

Eleven hours left.

Chapter 20

Rica's eyes searched mine, a mix of determination and doubt on her face. "Are you sure about this plan, Jack? We're diving into some dangerous territory."

I nodded, feeling the weight of the hours slipping away. "We don't have a choice. Time isn't on our side, and we've already spent two hours hashing this out. We need to locate Aeon and Jay quickly."

"Alright," she said, her voice steadying. "I can use my connections at the precinct to help find them. We can't afford to waste any more time."

"Perfect," I replied, my mind racing. "But I'll need some money to buy a few things for the plan. I promise I'll pay you back once this is all over."

Rica smirked, her arms crossing. "You better pay, Jack. I'm not a bank."

I chuckled despite the gravity of the situation. "Trust me, I will." We exchanged a nod of understanding before I continued, "I'll meet you at that bar in an hour after I get what I need."

With a quick parting, we separated, each of us with our own tasks.

One Hour Later

I entered the bar, a dimly lit place that had seen better days. Rica was already there, seated at a corner table with her phone in hand.

"Jack," she greeted, her expression brightening. "I've got some information on Aeon and Jay."

"Great!" I said, sliding into the seat opposite her. "I bought the burner phone. Let's start with Jay's number."

Rica nodded, pulling out her own phone. "Here. But let's run down the plan again to make sure we're on the same page."

"Right." I took a deep breath, focusing on the details. "First, we meet Aeon under the pretense that we're police officers investigating the accident. We'll say that while visiting the hospital, Jack woke up and asked the police to find the letter in his motorcycle to give it to Aeon before slipping back into a coma."

Rica listened intently. "And what's in the letter?"

I shrugged, feeling a little lost. "I dunno, I haven't figured out what to write yet, but I'll think of something."

Rica nodded, absorbing the strategy. "And the second task?"

"We'll trap Jay into confessing the fire he set at the gig venue," I explained, urgency creeping into my voice. "We'll text him that we know what he did and want to meet to discuss terms for keeping our mouths shut. I'll act while you're on standby to arrest him once he confesses."

Rica's eyes narrowed as she processed the plan. "We need to act fast. Only eight hours left."

I pulled out my burner phone, showing her the screen. "I already texted Jay. Now, we wait for a reply."

Minutes passed in tense silence, each second stretching into an eternity. The weight of the plan pressed down on me, and this was my chance for revenge—a chance to expose Jay for the monster he truly was. Memories of that night—the fire, the chaos, the innocent lives shattered—flashed through my mind, transporting me back to that fateful night.

The venue had been electric with energy. I could still hear the echoes of excitement, the crowd's cheers pulsating through the walls. We were on stage, our music reverberating, drawing everyone into a euphoric trance. I had turned to Dina, asking if she was ready. Her eyes sparkled with enthusiasm as she replied, "I can't wait to see you perform!" She was my biggest fan, and her support ignited my passion even more.

But as we began our set, a gnawing unease settled in. I scanned the sea of fans, searching for Dina, but she was nowhere to be found. The thrill of performing quickly turned to anxiety.

Suddenly, chaos erupted. A commotion broke out at the back of the crowd, and screams filled the air, piercing through the music like a knife. Panic surged as we realized the venue was on fire. My heart dropped. "Where's Dina?" I shouted, turning to Aeon and Jay. "Do you know where she is?"

They shook their heads, fear etched on their faces. "No, we don't know!"

"Get out!" I urged them. "You both need to leave now! I'll find her!"

With my heart pounding, I sprinted into the throng of panicking bodies, desperately searching for any sign of her. Confusion clouded my thoughts. Where could she be? What was I supposed to do?

Then, amidst the chaos, I heard a faint voice calling for help. "Help! Someone, please!"

The sound cut through the din, and I instinctively followed it, dread clawing at my insides. I ran toward the dressing room, my heart racing. As I reached the door, I froze. A chair had been wedged against it, trapping whoever was inside. I pushed against the door, forcing it open.

The sight before me was a nightmare. There lay Dina, crushed beneath a fallen pillar, her waist pinned down. Panic surged through me, and I rushed to her side, my hands trembling. "Dina!" I shouted, desperation clawing at my throat. "I'm here! I'm going to get you out!"

Tears streamed down her face, pain etched into every feature. "Jack... I can't move. It hurts!"

With all my strength, I tried to lift the pillar, but it was too heavy. "Hold on, Dina! I won't leave you! Just hold on!"

The heat from the flames pressed in around us, smoke filling the air. I felt like I was losing her, slipping away like the sound of the crowd that had once cheered for us.

But I couldn't give up. Not now. Not when she needed me most. I fought against the weight of the pillar, my muscles screaming in protest, praying for a miracle.

"Jack, please!" she cried, her voice strained.

"I'm here, Dina! I won't let you go!" I grunted as I pushed with every ounce of strength I had left, sweat pouring down my face.

It was a horrifying realization that I hadn't even considered until now. I thought at that time that it was just because of the falling debris that somehow wedged the chair against the door. Who would harbor such anger toward Dina that they would trap her inside a burning room?

But even as the anger simmered within me, I wrestled with my conscience. I couldn't bring myself to kill Jay, no matter how justified it might seem. I wouldn't stoop to his level; that was a line I refused to cross.

Arresting Jay was enough. I needed to let the law and justice take their course, ensuring he faced the consequences of his actions. But as I sat there, the tension coiling tighter in my chest, I wondered if I could truly stand by and let someone so vile continue to walk free.

Suddenly, the shrill beep of my burner phone broke through my thoughts, jolting me back to reality. The message lit up the screen, and my heart raced.

"It's Jay," I said, a mix of dread and excitement flooding me.

"Let's get this done," Rica urged, her voice steady.

I took a deep breath, feeling the weight of the moment settle over us. The clock was ticking, and we were about to dive headfirst into a dangerous game.

Rica's voice cut through the quiet. "Both of them are still at the office," she said, glancing at her phone. I checked the time—it was already 4 PM, just an hour before they clocked out.

I sighed, feeling the seconds slip through my fingers. Every moment mattered now, and yet, we had to wait. Rica suggested we confront Aeon only after she leaves the office, so Jay wouldn't see us. It made sense; if Jay caught sight of us hanging around, he'd be more cautious when we met him later. We needed him off guard, unsuspecting. I agreed, even though I felt the pressure of another wasted hour. But if it was for the greater good, I'd deal with it.

"We'll wait," I said. "In the meantime, I'll write the letter."

Easier said than done.

I settled back, pen poised over the notepad I'd brought, but my mind was blank. What could I possibly write that would make Aeon understand? Her feelings were so intense, so tangled. I didn't want to hurt her, but I couldn't keep pretending everything was fine. She needed to let go, move on. And I didn't know how to tell her that without shattering something inside her.

I glanced over at Rica, contemplating asking for her advice, but she shook her head, almost as if she read my mind. "It has to come from you," she said. "Only you can tell her what she needs to hear."

I gave a weak nod, even though I had no clue what that was. I tapped the pen against the page, trying to steady my thoughts.

I exhaled sharply, as if trying to blow away the thick fog in my head. This letter was my chance to fix that mistake, or at least try. I had to be honest, even if it hurt. There wasn't any other way. I started writing, letting the words flow, trying to find the balance between gratitude and finality. I wanted her to know how much her friendship meant to me, but I needed to make it clear that I could never give her what she wanted.

It felt like digging a knife into my own chest, knowing this might break her. But dragging it out any longer would only make it worse.

I was lost in the rhythm of the pen when Rica's voice snapped me back. "Are you done yet? We need to move; it's almost 5 PM."

I glanced at the letter, only half-finished. "I'll finish it on the way," I said, grabbing my stuff.

"Let's go."

We ended up at a coffee shop just across from Aeon's office building, a quaint little place with a rustic charm. The rich aroma of freshly brewed coffee filled the air, mingling with the sweet scent of pastries behind the glass display case. Soft jazz played in the background, creating a comforting atmosphere that felt oddly out of place given the tension in my chest.

The shop was adorned with dark wood furnishings and warm yellow lighting that cast a cozy glow over the small tables. We settled into a booth by the window, the glass fogged slightly from the warmth inside, offering a view of the bustling street. I remembered her once joking that it was her favorite place to unwind after a long day. I hoped she hadn't changed her routine.

Rica and I sat by the window, keeping an eye on the office doors. She was calm, but I could see the tension beneath her steady demeanor. We both knew what was at stake.

"Is Jay still texting?" she asked.

I pulled out my phone and checked. "Yeah," I said, scrolling through the messages. "But he's denying everything. Not taking the bait."

Rica nodded, like she expected as much. "Of course, he'll deny it. Try something stronger. Tell him we have evidence—CCTV footage from the venue."

I hesitated, then typed out the message. We have CCTV footage from that night. It even caught you wedging the chair on the dressing room door.

I hit send, hoping it would push him over the edge. "Done."

Rica gave a small, satisfied smile. "The bait's been recast. Let's see if the fish will finally bite."

I nodded, but my attention was drifting to the entrance of the office across the street. My heart skipped a beat when I saw Aeon stepping out, her bag slung over her shoulder, looking down at her phone as she crossed the street. She was completely oblivious to what was waiting for her on this side.

I felt a knot tighten in my chest. I knew what I had to do, but knowing didn't make it any easier. I glanced at Rica, and she nodded, giving me a silent "go ahead."

I took a deep breath, trying to steady the tremble in my hands. This was it—the moment of truth. For Aeon, for Jay, for everything.

Time Left: 7 Hours

Chapter 21

As I sat in the coffee shop across from Aeon's office, the warm aroma of freshly brewed coffee filled the air, but my focus was solely on her. I watched as Aeon stepped up to the counter, placing her order with the barista, her expression a mix of concentration and anticipation. She looked just as I remembered—intelligent and driven—but now there was an undeniable distance between us that felt insurmountable.

Rica and I exchanged glances, both of us patiently waiting for Aeon to receive her coffee and dessert. After what felt like an eternity, Aeon finally picked up her order and made her way to a corner table, where she settled in, scrolling through her phone.

"Now's our chance," Rica said, squeezing my hand gently.

I nodded, but as we approached her, my heart raced. Why was it so hard to move? I had always talked to her so casually, yet now it felt like a padlock had locked my lips shut.

Rica stepped beside me, a determined look in her eyes. "Excuse me, Miss," she said brightly as we reached Aeon's table.

Aeon looked up, surprised, her brows knitting together in curiosity. "Yes? Can I help you?"

"I'm Investigator Rica Santos," Rica introduced herself, her tone firm yet friendly. She flashed her badge with confidence. "I'm with the task force assigned to investigate the incident involving Jack S. Jacques." She gestured to me. "And this is my partner, Enzo Santos."

The surname caught me off guard. Santos? So Enzo's last name was Santos? I hadn't connected the dots before, and now I found myself wondering about Rica's relationship with him as I stood frozen, trying to process everything.

"Sorry about him," Rica added with a light chuckle, glancing at me with a playful smile. "He's... a bit shy."

I felt my cheeks flush, trapped in silence as I struggled to gather my thoughts. How was I supposed to talk to her now, with my heart pounding in my chest?

"Don't worry, I don't bite," Aeon replied with a light laugh, her flirtatious tone snapping me back to reality.

Finally, I found my voice, an urgency driving me forward. "Can you tell us what you recall from your last meeting with Jack?"

Aeon's brow furrowed as she thought. "We were having drinks at a bar with friends. He left early to buy ice cream for his wife, Dina." Her tone was casual, but I could hear the underlying affection she still felt for me.

"Did Jack mention anything about giving you something?" I pressed, trying to mask my rising anxiety.

"Um, no, nothing specific," she said, a hint of confusion in her voice.

I knew I had to pivot, to create a plausible story that would allow me to deliver the letter. "While visiting the hospital, Jack woke up briefly and asked the police to find a letter in his motorcycle to give to you before slipping back into a coma."

The shock registered on her face. "A letter?"

I nodded, pulling out the letter I had prepared. "Here it is." I handed it to her, my heart pounding as she took it, her fingers trembling slightly.

Aeon wasted no time opening the letter, her eyes scanning the words. "Hey Aeon," she began to read aloud, her voice steady but slowly faltering with each line:

"I'm putting this down on paper 'cause I can't bring myself to say this to your face. It's easier to hide behind words than to see the hurt in your eyes. You've been a bright spot in my life, always there with a laugh and a kind word. But I can't keep pretending I feel the same way. The truth is, I just don't love you the way you deserve. You deserve someone who can light up your world, not someone who's constantly falling short."

Her voice trembled, and I could see the devastation washing over her. "No... No, he can't mean this." Her eyes lingered on the letter, as though staring hard enough might change the words on the page. She gripped it tighter, her knuckles turning white.

I watched as she read the lines over and over, her lips moving silently, as though searching for any trace of warmth, of something that might reveal this was all a mistake—a sick joke or a misunderstanding. Her shoulders started to shake, and she pressed her hand to her mouth, blinking back tears. It seemed like she was trying to hold herself together, to force herself to breathe even as every word felt like it was tearing her apart.

As she continued reading, the air felt heavy with unspoken emotions. I hesitated, not knowing how to comfort her but feeling compelled to try. "Aeon, I—"

She cut me off, tears brimming in her eyes. "He really doesn't love me? After everything we shared?"

"It's—" I paused, searching for the right words. "It's clear he's trying to protect you from more pain. Sometimes, friendship can't fill the gaps left by love. It's hard to see someone we care about struggle, but being honest is a way to show you truly care."

Aeon bit her lip, tears spilling down her cheeks as she finished the letter. "I thought... I thought we had something real."

"It's okay to feel hurt," I said, unsure but wanting to reassure her. "Jack cared about you, and it sounds like he valued your friendship. But he also wanted to make sure you find someone who can give you what you deserve."

She looked at me, a mixture of heartbreak and confusion in her gaze.

"I know it's painful," I continued, "Just give yourself time to process it. You deserve to be loved fully, and that will happen for you, I promise."

Aeon nodded slowly, her gaze drifting to the letter in her hands. "Thank you for bringing this to me," she murmured, her voice a fragile whisper. "I just wish... I wish it didn't hurt so much."

I reached out, placing a comforting hand on her shoulder. "I know it's painful. Just give yourself time to process it. You deserve to be loved fully, and that will happen for you, I promise."

Aeon looked down, her expression thoughtful as she processed my words. The silence hung between us, heavy with unspoken feelings. I could see her wrestling with the weight of the moment, and I sensed it was time to wrap up our meeting.

Suddenly, my phone buzzed softly in my pocket, interrupting the moment. I glanced at the screen, my heart quickening as I read Jay's message: "Got him! He's taking the bait."

I felt a rush of urgency but also a pang of guilt for the timing. "I'm really sorry, Miss," I said gently, turning back to her. "We have to go. Rica and I need to handle something important."

She blinked, surprise flickering across her face. "Oh... okay. Is everything alright?"

"Yeah, it's just business. But you'll be okay, right?" I asked, hoping to reassure her.

She gave me a small smile, though it didn't quite reach her eyes. "Yeah, I'll be fine. Just... give yourself time, too, Jack."

Rica shot a quick glance at me, then back at Aeon, her smile brightening the mood. "Don't worry, Aeon. There are plenty of fish in the sea," she said cheerfully, her tone reassuring.

I could see Aeon take a deep breath, her expression softening a bit at Rica's words. "Thanks, I guess. I just didn't expect this," she replied, her voice still tinged with sadness.

Rica nodded understandingly. "I get that. But sometimes, it's about finding the right fish, you know? You deserve someone who sees your worth."

I glanced at my phone again, the urgency of Jay's message creeping back into my mind. "I'm really sorry, Aeon, but Rica and I have to go handle something," I said, trying to sound as gentle as possible.

Aeon nodded slowly, a hint of acceptance in her eyes. "Yeah, I understand. You guys go take care of it. Thanks for giving me this," she said, lifting the letter slightly in her hand. The gesture felt both heavy and hopeful, a silent acknowledgment of her pain and the possibility of moving forward.

I glanced at Rica, who gave me an encouraging nod. "Take care of yourself, Aeon," I said softly. "And remember, it's okay to feel whatever you're feeling right now."

As we turned to leave, Rica added with a playful smile, "Just remember, the sea is vast and full of possibilities. Don't lose hope!"

As we stepped out, the cool air wrapped around us like a welcome embrace. It was already 6 PM, but beneath that refreshing chill lay a knot of unease in my stomach. I took a moment to inhale deeply, letting the brisk air fill my lungs as I tried to shake off the weight of our conversation with Aeon. The second task was looming, another emotional roller coaster that I wasn't quite ready to face. Yet, with time running out, I had to muster the strength to persevere.

After a moment of silence, I pulled out my phone, the familiar weight of it grounding me. Rica glanced at me, her expression curious. "So, what did Jay say?" she asked, her tone a mix of concern and anticipation.

"He wants to meet at a bar," I replied, my heart racing at the thought of what was to come. I read the message again, my brow furrowing. "He sent the coordinates and wants to meet at 11 PM. He insists that I come alone."

"That's too close to the deadline," Rica said, urgency creeping into her voice.

"I know," I replied, feeling the weight of the situation settle on my shoulders. "But with that much spare time, we can prepare the venue to catch him."

With a final look back at the coffee shop, I steeled myself for what lay ahead. We had less than six hours, and the second task was looming—another emotional roller coaster that I wasn't quite ready to face.

But as we walked toward our next destination, I knew I had to muster the strength to persevere. Whatever awaited us, I couldn't turn back now.

6 hours left...

Chapter 22

As we drove toward the venue, a heavy silence settled between us, broken only by the hum of the engine. I couldn't shake the growing sense of unease creeping into my bones, like a slow, crawling chill. Eight hours had passed since I took over Enzo's body, and with each hour, the symptoms of death were getting harder to ignore. My limbs felt like they were weighed down by something unseen, and my movements grew stiffer, as though rigor mortis was lurking just beneath the surface.

I caught myself staring into the rearview mirror, drawn in by my own reflection. Enzo's face looked back at me—pale and shadowed in the car's dim interior. The truth of my situation was settling in, and with it, a faint, unmistakable odor was beginning to cling to me, something stale and earthy that belonged six feet under, not in a car on the way to a gig venue. I cringed, realizing it was more noticeable than I thought, and maybe a breath mint was the least of my concerns.

Beside me, Rica glanced over, her brow furrowing. I expected concern, maybe disgust. But instead, a smirk spread across her face, softening the tension in her features. "Hey," she joked, voice light with that signature touch of sarcasm, "you smell like a morgue." Her tone held that mix of humor and compassion I was starting to recognize. She leaned toward me, rummaging through her bag with a casual confidence I was grateful for. "How about a little perfume?" She pulled out a small spray bottle and wiggled it between her fingers, a mischievous twinkle in her eye. "I promise, it's not just for my benefit," she continued, her tone lowering in mock seriousness. "I'd rather not have you eating my brains later."

I let out a laugh, one I didn't know I was holding in, feeling the tension in my shoulders ease a bit. Even as I waved away the thought of actually spraying perfume over this persistent odor, her humor lightened the grimness. "Thanks, but I'll pass on the brains for now," I replied, my words laced with irony. For the first time since I took on this borrowed life, I felt a sliver of normalcy creep in—a reminder that even in the strangest situations, someone like Rica could find a way to keep things real.

But as the laughter faded, the energy between us shifted. I glanced over at her, noting the way her expression changed, growing thoughtful, her fingers gripping the steering wheel a little tighter. It was as though she was carrying something far heavier than any one person should. I sensed she was gathering her thoughts, bracing herself to share something that had stayed buried until now.

"Jack..." she started, her voice soft, hesitant. There was a weight in her tone that caught me off guard, drawing me closer to the moment. "There's something I need to tell you about Enzo."

Her words hung in the air, quiet but intense, sending a rush of curiosity through me. I turned toward her, trying to read the subtle emotions playing across her face. "What is it?"

Rica took a slow, measured breath, her gaze fixed on the road ahead. I could see her jaw clench as she braced herself, the effort it took to bring her thoughts into words. "Enzo was my husband," she said, her voice barely above a whisper, yet the confession hit with the weight of a thunderclap. "He... he died of cardiac arrest."

I felt a pang of shock ripple through me, and for a moment, the reality of my situation shifted in a way I hadn't expected. Here I was, borrowing the life of a man who had been Rica's whole world—a man she was still mourning. The air grew thick with the unspoken, and I couldn't help but feel a strange sense of trespass, as if I'd stumbled into a sacred space not meant for me. I glanced at her, unsure of what to say, but feeling her pain resonate deeply within me.

She seemed to sense my silence, so she offered more, as if speaking about him would lessen the ache. "What was he like?" I asked, gently, wanting her to know I was listening, that I understood how much it meant.

Rica's lips curved into a faint smile, bittersweet and touched with a longing that reached back into her memories. Her eyes softened, the sadness mingling with the warmth of something beautiful. "Enzo was the kindest person I ever knew," she began, her words brimming with affection. "He had this incredible way of making everyone feel special. He always knew how to make me laugh, no matter how bad my day was."

There was a distant look in her eyes as if she could still see him, hear his laugh, feel the warmth of his presence beside her. She continued, her voice laced with nostalgia. "We had this perfect date just yesterday before he died. It was the two of us at our favorite restaurant. He knew exactly what to order for me, even before I could say a word. And when we were done, he surprised me by taking me to the park."

She paused, a small, fond laugh escaping her lips. "He knew I loved being outdoors at night, under the stars. He'd packed a blanket, and we just sat there, laughing and talking for hours. It felt like a scene from a movie." Her voice grew softer, filled with a tenderness that made the car feel smaller, as if we were sharing an intimate moment from her past. "He looked at me that night as though I was the only person in the world. We talked about our dreams, our future, all the little things that made us happy. He made me feel... complete."

I listened, struck by the simplicity and purity of what they shared. It was a love that needed no embellishments, no grand gestures—it was built on shared moments, laughter, and the way they could just be together. I could see the weight of her loss, the way it pulled at her with each word, yet somehow, she seemed grateful to share it with someone. I didn't dare interrupt her, didn't dare break the spell of her memories.

"But then," her voice cracked slightly, and I felt the shift—the beautiful memory turning, the pain and shock twisting her words. "It all changed in an instant. Right there, in the middle of our laughter, he... he just collapsed in front of me." She swallowed hard, her fingers white-knuckled on the wheel. "I didn't even realize what was happening. One second, he was laughing, and the next... I couldn't comprehend it. I couldn't do anything but watch as he..."

Her voice trailed off, the silence between us filled with her pain. I felt a sharp pang of sympathy, her sorrow carving a deep ache in the space between us. I wanted to say something, anything, to comfort her, but words felt useless in the face of such profound loss.

"I'm so sorry, Rica," I managed, my voice low. The words felt inadequate, but it was all I could offer.

She nodded, blinking back the tears that threatened to fall. "Thank you, Jack." Her voice was barely audible, but the gratitude in it was real. She took a shaky breath, her gaze focused on the road ahead as she collected herself. "I remember his smile, the way he'd make these silly jokes just to see me laugh. We'd even planned a trip to the beach together, a weekend getaway to escape everything, just the two of us. And now... now he's gone."

The depth of her grief was palpable, and I could feel the weight of the emptiness that Enzo had left behind. The silence stretched, both of us lost in the gravity of what she had just shared. It wasn't just a story—it was her life, her love, and the wound that she carried with her every day.

"That's why I need to talk to Sidapa," she said after a long pause, her voice suddenly filled with determination. There was a fire in her eyes now, a fierce glint that replaced the sorrow, though it didn't erase it. "Maybe he can bring the real Enzo back to life. I just... I can't let go of the hope that I might see him again, that maybe he's out there, waiting."

I nodded slowly, feeling the gravity of her words sink in. "Let's make sure we get that chance, Rica," I said, my voice filled with the resolve I hadn't felt before. "We'll do whatever it takes."

Rica looked at me, a glimmer of gratitude in her gaze, though I could still see the lingering pain in her eyes. "Thank you, Jack. I know it's a lot to ask, but I just can't shake the feeling that there's still something left to be done."

As she spoke, I could hear the tremor in her voice, a subtle crack that betrayed the strength she was trying to project. It was as if she was balancing on the edge of her emotions, and I felt a tug at my heart. Just for a moment, her gaze dropped to her hands gripping the steering wheel, and I noticed the faint glimmer of tears in her eyes, a reflection of her unyielding pain.

"Rica..." I started, but the weight of her sorrow made my words catch in my throat.

"She quickly wiped her eyes, as if to shield me from her grief, but I had already seen enough. The façade of strength crumbled just enough to reveal the raw hurt beneath. My heart ached for her, the realization hitting me hard—she was not just mourning her husband; she was also carrying the burden of a future snatched away too soon.

"Let's make sure we get that chance, Rica. We'll do whatever it takes." My voice came out firmer than I felt, but I needed her to hear my resolve.

As we neared the venue, I took a deep breath, trying to gather my thoughts. "Alright, here's the plan..."

Chapter 23

The pub was packed, its air thick with a blend of smoke, chatter, and the hum of an evening crowd oblivious to what was about to unfold. Rica moved through the dimly lit room, her gaze meeting those of the undercover officers subtly positioned among the patrons. They looked like any other group of friends out for drinks, laughing and bantering as they nursed half-full beers. But beneath their jackets, each one was wired, a listening device in place, tuned to catch every word that spilled from Jay's mouth.

Near the back, I found a seat across from Jay, whose eyes flashed with a hint of suspicion as I sat down. He didn't know who I really was, of course. To him, I was just some guy who'd "witnessed" things better left forgotten, things that could cost him if I were to talk. He took a slow drag on his cigarette, sizing me up.

"So, what's it gonna be?" he asked, his tone impatient. "You want money to keep your mouth shut, is that it?"

I played my part, letting a smirk stretch across Enzo's face as I leaned back in the booth. "Something like that," I replied, keeping my tone casual. "The way I see it, you owe me for the trouble." I watched as he relaxed, if only slightly, thinking he could buy his way out. But as the minutes ticked by, I subtly pushed the conversation closer to the truth.

A flash of Rica's face crossed my mind—the serious, determined look she'd worn as she briefed the officers earlier. We'd planned this to the second, making sure everything was set for this one shot. She'd assigned each officer their position and instructed them on what to do once Jay confessed. We needed him to admit his crime, clearly and explicitly, to be sure it would hold up in court.

Back at the table, Jay's smile had turned smug, thinking he'd bought my silence. "You don't know what happened that night," he muttered, his voice a low hiss. "You're just some idiot in over his head."

"I know enough, Jay. I know about the fire, about the person who died because of it," I said, leaning forward. My voice dropped to a lethal whisper. "I know you're the one who lit the match... and that you locked an innocent woman in the dressing room that night."

Jay froze, a flicker of panic flashing across his face. He looked around, but the pub was too full, too loud—no one seemed to be paying attention. He laughed it off, though his confidence faltered. "You got it all wrong," he said, his voice wavering just enough to betray him.

But I wasn't letting him off that easily. "You mean to tell me you didn't do it?" I asked, my tone almost mocking. "The fire just started itself?"

Jay's face contorted with anger, his hands clenched into fists. For a moment, I thought he'd lash out, but then he leaned back, the faintest smirk appearing on his lips. "So what if I did?" he muttered under his breath, almost to himself. "So what if I took care of a few things? It was just a dump anyway, and some people need to learn to mind their own business."

In a nearby flashback, Rica had rehearsed exactly how this would go down. She'd said to give Jay time to let his guard slip, to let the truth spill out on its own. We'd both known he'd eventually brag about his crime, unable to keep his pride and arrogance in check. And sure enough, here he was, gloating over the fire as if it were some badge of honor.

The listening devices picked up every word, transmitting them back to the officers who were now slowly moving in, surrounding our booth. Jay hadn't noticed yet. He was still riding the high of his confession, grinning as he relished the memory of the fire. It was only when I raised my hand, signaling the officers, that he realized something was off.

"What's going on?" he hissed, glancing around as the officers closed in. Panic flashed across his face as he saw Rica approaching, handcuffs in hand. His smile vanished, replaced by fury and desperation.

"You're under arrest, Jay," Rica said firmly, her tone as cold as steel.

He glared at her, rage twisting his features. "You set me up!"

Jay tried to lunge at me, but I sidestepped, letting him stumble into the waiting arms of the officers. They restrained him, securing his wrists in the cuffs as he thrashed and spat curses. The adrenaline coursed through me, the satisfaction of having finally brought him to justice settling in.

As they hauled Jay to his feet, I could feel a sense of calm wash over me. It was done. My task was complete, and with two minutes to spare. I'd finally be able to see Dina again, to rest beside her in peace. A bittersweet smile tugged at my lips as I glanced around the room, knowing this was likely my last moment here. I could already feel myself beginning to slip away, my grip on Enzo's body loosening as the clock ran out.

"Dina..." I whispered, my voice barely audible, savoring the thought of seeing her smile, of finding peace at last.

But then, everything shattered in an instant.

Jay, with a sudden burst of strength, twisted his body, yanking one of the officers off balance. In the chaos, his hand shot toward Rica's holstered gun, his fingers wrapping around it before anyone could react. I saw his arm swing up, the barrel of the gun aimed right at her chest.

"Rica!" I shouted, lunging toward her, but it was too late.

The shot echoed through the pub, and Rica staggered back, clutching her side. Blood seeped between her fingers, and she gasped, her face pale with shock. I barely had a second to register it before Jay turned the gun on me, pulling the trigger again. A searing pain shot through my chest, and I felt my knees buckle as I collapsed to the floor.

Time slowed as I lay there, the sounds around me fading into a distant hum. I could see Rica's face above me, her expression a mixture of shock and pain. She was struggling to stay conscious, her hand still pressed to her wound as she fought to hold on.

My vision dimmed, the edges blurring as the pain faded, giving way to an unexpected, settling calm. This wasn't the end I'd imagined, but maybe it was enough. The last thing I saw was the sorrow in Rica's eyes, her voice a soft, distant echo whispering my name.

Then... only silence.

Epilogue

A heartbeat later, the silence gave way to a subtle hum, and I felt myself lifted, suspended in a space that defied the world of the living. Dark mist swirled around me, and the air pulsed with a powerful, ancient energy. As I steadied myself, Sidapa appeared before me, exuding a calm authority that cut through the fog and stillness.

"Congratulations, Jack," he said, his voice reverberating through the strange, twilight space. "You've accomplished your task."

I paused, disoriented. "What... What happened after I was shot?"

Sidapa's expression remained neutral. "The undercover officers were ready. They took Jay down as soon as he pulled the trigger."

A swirl of emotions swept over me—anger, relief, and a strange emptiness. After everything, I had finally completed my mission, and a peace settled within me. In just moments, I would be with Dina, leaving behind this world of pain and loss. But then a thought crossed my mind, one that twisted in my chest.

"And... What about Rica?" I asked.

Before Sidapa could respond, a familiar voice cut through the dim space, echoing in a mixture of awe and certainty. "Are you Sidapa?" Rica's voice, clear and steady, broke through.

My heart skipped. I turned, feeling a jolt of confusion as I saw her standing just a few feet away. She looked the same as ever, though there was a stillness in her, as if she, too, was caught between worlds.

Sidapa turned toward her, an almost imperceptible nod acknowledging her presence. "Yes, I am. And I am well aware of the role you played in Jack's task. You performed it admirably," he said, a hint of respect in his tone. "I know you sought to speak with me, so speak freely."

Rica's eyes flickered with hope, the desire she had carried in silence now at the forefront. "Can you... can you return Enzo's soul to this world? So can we live together again, in peace?"

Sidapa's gaze softened, but he shook his head slowly. "Enzo's soul has moved beyond the reach of this realm and entered the afterlife. He is no longer retrievable." He paused, watching the hope in Rica's expression transform to a solemn acceptance. "However, you deserve a reward for what you've done. So, I grant you two choices."

She listened intently, her body still and tense.

"You are, indeed, dead," Sidapa explained, his voice gentle but firm. "Jay's bullet ended your life. But I can return your soul, allowing you to live a peaceful life among the living." He paused, letting the weight of his words settle. "Or, if you prefer, I can reunite your soul with Enzo's, allowing you both to spend eternity together."

Rica's answer was immediate, her voice unwavering. "I choose the second option."

Sidapa nodded in acknowledgment, a hint of something like admiration in his gaze. "Love and loyalty like yours deserve honor," he said, his words carrying a deep reverence. "The bonds we forge and the sacrifices we make in life create the threads that shape our souls. You, Rica, embody the rare courage to honor those bonds even beyond death."

She looked at Sidapa, then back at me. "Enzo was... everything," she said softly. "Every time he'd come home from work, even on the hardest days, he'd bring me a flower. It didn't matter if it was a beautiful rose or a random wildflower he'd found on the street; to him, it was a symbol. He'd always say, 'So you'll know I thought of you today.'" Her voice trembled as she recounted the memory, her eyes reflecting the happiness and quiet devotion she'd shared with Enzo. "After he died, it felt like... like every part of me was gone with him."

My throat tightened, my own words catching as I saw the depths of what she was giving up. "Rica, you're stronger than anyone I know. I know it's not fair to ask you to stay, but I want you to know... you were there for me through every step of this task I walked through. Thank you."

She smiled at me, a quiet, grateful smile. "Jack, I think you would have done the same if it were you. You're good, in your own way. Keep going. I know you'll find what you're looking for."

A lump formed in my throat, and I nodded, my respect for her deepening. Sidapa gave a final nod, acknowledging her choice with the solemnity of a vow.

"Then so be it," he intoned, lifting a hand in blessing as a gentle light surrounded Rica. She looked at me one last time, her gaze holding gratitude, peace, and a quiet farewell. Then, as if carried by the air itself, her figure faded, her spirit now joined with Enzo's, free to spend eternity where her heart truly belonged.

Sidapa turned back to me, his eyes reflecting something deeper—a quiet satisfaction, as though he, too, felt the justice in Rica's reward.

"Now, Jack," he began, his voice echoing through the strange realm, carrying both warmth and gravity. "Are you ready to return to your own body?"

The words hit me, sharper than I expected. After all I'd gone through—being yanked into a world where my favorite band didn't even exist, from a life of fame to a world that had moved on without me. I'd watched Dina die, felt the agony of losing her, and then I'd died—three times over, each one more brutal than the last. I'd been thrown into a stranger's dead body, broken the heart of a girl I was close to since college.

It felt impossible to think of "going back" after all that. Would it even feel like my life anymore? And could I even call myself the same Jack who had walked away from it all in the first place?

But standing in Sidapa's gaze, the questions gave way to a different, calmer certainty, a strange sense of purpose.

I took a deep breath, the heaviness in my chest lifting as I looked into Sidapa's eyes, feeling the weight of my journey settle around me. "I'm ready," I replied, my voice steady, the finality of my words echoing in the twilight space.

Sidapa nodded, a solemn smile creeping onto his face. "Then, Jack, you may return."

With that, the world around me blurred, the dark mist swirling faster until everything faded into a brilliant light. It enveloped me, and for a moment, I felt weightless, suspended between realms.

And then, I fell again.

When I opened my eyes, the light was replaced by the soft glow of a hospital room. Blinking against the brightness, I registered the familiar beeping of machines and the muted sounds of nurses chatting in the hallway.

My gaze shifted down to see her—Dina—curled up beside my leg on the bed, her features relaxed in peaceful slumber. Relief washed over me, a wave of emotions crashing against the shore of my heart. She was here. After everything, she was here.

In the background, the gentle strumming of a familiar melody floated through the air—a soothing tune that brought a sense of calm and nostalgia. "Di Na Muli" played softly on the radio, weaving its way through my consciousness, echoing the love and loss that had marked my journey.

"Dina," I whispered, the name escaping my lips like a prayer. I reached out, brushing my fingers against her hair, feeling the warmth of her presence grounding me in this moment.

And as the song played on, I knew I was finally home.

www.ingramcontent.com/pod-product-compliance
Lightning Source LLC
Chambersburg PA
CBHW071002180726
48291CB00004B/1399